BY GEORGE SAUNDERS

Fiction

CivilWarLand in Bad Decline
Pastoralia
The Very Persistent Gappers of Frip
The Brief and Frightening Reign of Phil
In Persuasion Nation
Tenth of December
Fox 8
Lincoln in the Bardo
Liberation Day
Vigil

Nonfiction

The Braindead Megaphone
Congratulations, by the Way
A Swim in a Pond in the Rain

Vigil

Vigil

A NOVEL

George Saunders

RANDOM HOUSE | NEW YORK

Random House
An imprint and division of Penguin Random House LLC
1745 Broadway, New York, NY 10019
randomhousebooks.com
penguinrandomhouse.com

Hardcover ISBN 9780525509622
Ebook ISBN 9780525509639

Printed in the United States of America

1st Printing

FIRST EDITION

BOOK TEAM: Production editor: Evan Camfield • Managing editor: Rebecca Berlant • Production manager: Richard Elman • Copy editor: Bonnie Thompson • Proofreaders: Chuck Thompson, Tricia Wygal

Book design by Simon M. Sullivan

The authorized representative in the EU for product safety and compliance is Penguin Random House Ireland, Morrison Chambers, 32 Nassau Street, Dublin D02 YH68, Ireland. https://eu-contact.penguin.ie

To Paula (this one, especially)

Vigil

What a lovely home I found myself plummeting toward, acquiring, as I fell, arms, hands, legs, feet, all of which, as usual, became more substantial with each passing second.

Below: a fountain.

At the center of the fountain: a gold-plated statue.

Of a dog. (Someone must have really loved that dog.)

In the mouth of the golden dog: a golden duck. The duck's beak was hanging open in death and a pocked area in its flank seemed meant to represent the entry-field of the shot-cluster.

I observed all of this as I plummeted past and then my head and torso pierced the asphalt crust of a semicircular drive and lodged in the dirt below.

My rear was in the air, my fresh new legs bicycling energetically. I found myself alternately clothed and unclothed. That is to say: one instant naked and the next clothed. Or to be more precise: partly clothed. (Over time, that is, the elements of my outfit grew more reliably visible.)

My beige skirt soon became a near constant.

Meanwhile, here was a burrowing worm to consider and a brown bottle-shard and the rich smell of the loam now completely encasing my (inverted) upper half.

Once in Tennessee, having landed in the more conventional upright posture, I spent six hours in a paddock, my head protruding above the surface of the earth, being trotted through again and again by three black horses and one roan, who never, during those hours, ceased being panicked by my presence.

And yet I had a fine success on that occasion.

My charge being greatly comforted.

Tonight, blessedly, the thaw proceeded quickly.

And I found myself able, by sheer force of will, to bolt up out of the ground gymnastically and stand upright, both fully and consistently clothed.

Beige skirt, pale pink blouse, black pumps.

The golden dog shone in the glare of an ornate carriage lamp.

I made for the front door and, not yet walking competently, collapsed to the earth like a just-unstrung puppet, then leapt to my feet and moved on relentlessly to my work.

The door (immense, heavy, dead-bolted) presented no meaningful impediment. Passing through, I emerged into a magnificent entryway, then ascended a spacious stairwell lined with image after image of my charge:

Leaning confidently against a podium, speaking to a tremendous crowd.

Squatting with a kaffiyeh-wearing fellow before the Great Pyramid of Giza.

Knee-deep in the shallows of some high mountain lake, beside a young woman I took to be his daughter.

Driving (pretending to drive) a piece of heavy machinery, wearing a hard hat and a three-piece suit.

Posing before an oil rig.

And another.

And another.

Standing with his wife on the Great Wall of China, both beaming as if this represented a singular moment in their union.

Arm in arm with her in what looked to be the Rose Garden of the White House.

With her again, before what I understood to be a second home, in Colorado.

And a third, in Hawaii.

A fourth, in Key West.

Often, on his face, the same look: more grimace than smile, albeit shot through with a measure of forced goodwill.

Reaching the second floor, I moved along a hallway hung with numerous paintings in gilt frames, each marked by a plaque mentioning some experience our charge and his wife associated with its acquisition:

"Lovely cliffside dinner, Positano."

"Catacomb tour, Paris, Mr. Pavarotti sang beautifully for us after dinner."

"Guest of Senator Jepps and Maria in their fabulous desert home."

At the end of the hall hung a double door of sturdy oak.

A familiar tan purse now appearing over my shoulder, I patted it (once, twice) as I would in the bygone days when about to embark on a challenging task, then passed through, knowing that my charge must be found on the other side.

And here he was.

A tiny, crimped fellow in an immense mahogany bed.

I was not too late.

Neither was I too early.

His wife, exhausted by care, slept fully dressed on a love seat near the bed. Her slippers lay on the floor, turned in toward each other as if being worn by some invisible pigeon-toed individual.

But she was not my concern.

My charge's sleeping clothes were of silk, his initials monogrammed above the heart.

Moving closer, I entered the orb of his thoughts.

Within him abided a formidable stubbornness. A steady flow of satisfaction, even triumph, coursed through him, regarding all he had managed to do, see, cause, and create, especially given his humble origins.

I scanned for doubts regarding things he had done or left undone; things he might have said but had not; mistakes to which he had not yet fully admitted, any of which might keep him from attaining that state of total peace so to be desired at this juncture.

And found nothing, or nearly nothing.

He was as sure of himself as ever a charge of mine had been.

Even now, as the terrible illness overtook him.

I felt again the old, familiar, generalized fondness:

Before me lay a person who had not willed himself into this

world and was now being taken out of it by force, the many subsystems within him that had always given him so much satisfaction shutting down agonizingly. Soon *it* would come, accompanied by disbelief and panic, and he would find himself on the wrong side of a rapidly closing door, everything he had ever known and loved out of reach, over *there,* beyond it.

At such moments, I especially cherished my task.

I could comfort.

I could.

I moved to the window to energize and activate that part of myself from which I comforted, by glimpsing out indulgently at the glory of all-that-is.

To my surprise, down below, near the statue of the golden dog, stood one of our ilk, looking up.

He must be one of us, for he seemed able to see me.

And began beseeching me, by way of a complicated series of gestures, to indulge him, by exiting the home and floating down for a quick word, if I would be so kind.

I passed out through the wall, the stale quiet of the death room giving way to the smell of the humid air without and the lovely nighttime sound of cicadas, all my clothes now properly affixed and permanent, a happy development, since I must now greet this new acquaintance.

The fellow appeared exhausted, as if he had traveled a great distance to be here. Wearing the rough garb of a mechanic or railway engineer, he struggled under the weight of a tremendous stack of papers, the top of which was invisible among the low-hanging midsummer clouds. Its great height causing the stack to exist in a continual state of sway, he must, to prevent it from toppling, continuously be adjusting his posture.

He was indeed one of us.

For I could see, through his body, the trunk of an oak across the street.

He implored me, in fluent but accented English: Might I allow him up into that room, briefly, as a courtesy? *Est-il possible?* He understood that this might represent an inconvenient interruption of my work. Which, perhaps, had not yet begun in earnest? He possessed certain information he felt would prove beneficial. To my charge. Also, if he was being entirely transparent—

You are, I said. Entirely.

We shared a laugh.

If I am being entirely *frank*, he restated, it would benefit me as well. I would be most grateful. I assure you I will do no harm: *Je vous promets.*

His forlorn appearance engaged my compassion. His clothing was in tatters, he was filthy with the dust of the road, his shoes mere flaps of leather, his feet blistered and bloody.

And, if possible, he said, I would prefer to go up alone.

Alone, I said.

S'il vous plaît, he said.

It was an immense task we of our ilk were engaged upon. We constituted a guild of sorts, that depended for its work upon such mutual gestures of courtesy.

I indicated with a slight inclination of my head that I would allow it.

Kindly be quick, I said.

Up the Frenchman leapt, showing a surprising agility for one so burdened, his immense stack of papers seeming to inhibit him not a bit.

From the backyard of the house next door came a burst of music and the low murmur of a crowd.

A party, it seemed.

Seated on the edge of the fountain, hearing these sounds (my task suspended, entering a dangerous, purpose-free state of lull), I began to experience familiar symptoms of an affliction that, when upon me, always caused me to become less powerful and effective than was desirable.

For example:

Near the golden statue, in a swath of tree-created moon-shadow, was what I knew, of the instant, to be "auto." I myself, I recalled, had, in that previous realm, driven several "autos," the first of which had been "Chevelle." "Chevelle," packed with "girlfriends," as well as my cousin, "Steve," would be positioned so as to face a "movie-film" unscrolling upon a distant wall of white, surrounded by other autos, all of us learning from the movie-film such things as: Rome is romantic and interesting. And: when someone is lovely, the household staff may exchange happy glances regarding one's sunny insouciance. And: later, those servants will help one achieve one's fondest dreams, by keeping one's confidence regarding a secret rendezvous.

All of this, just because one was lovely.

Therefore, sitting in Chevelle, watching those movie-films, I wished to be lovely.

Was I?

Had I been?

At this remove, I couldn't recall. I could only recall dear Chevelle and those movie-films and my aspiration to be lovely.

More such recollections would soon be forthcoming.

Though they were harmful.

Ugh.

Here came one now:

I am digging away at the surface of "school desk" with the point of "compass" from "Sears" as "Mrs. Kiley" drones on. The lesson, as always, eludes me. What I want is to go home and play "PrettyPetals." That, at least, I am good at. Through a nearby window (so close I might reach over and touch it, if I dared, which I don't), three children too young for school play among gently swaying "swing set" seats. Lucky ducks! Butterflies dart about, seemingly more quickly or slowly in proportion to the joy in the children's voices.

The more joy, the more agitated the butterflies.

Darn.

Darn it.

To my chagrin, I now recalled:

"Jill."

"Jill Blaine."

"Jill 'Doll' Blaine."

In the bygone days, that (alas) had been me.

Sitting on the edge of the fountain, I resisted several additional recollections:

The feeling of toting in two bags of "groceries," one in each arm; the "glassclunk" (one, then the second) as these are set down in sequence.

No, no, no.

Dangling one's feet in the "new aboveground pool" as crazy light-stars danced across the surface of the "heavily chlorinated water." Having "hopped right in," one felt, through "plastic liner," one's footprints imprinting upon the soft swells of underlying sand.

Oh gosh, oh dear.

Surely that Frenchman must be done by now.

I vaulted up, passed through the bedroom wall, found him standing on the bed sweating profusely, treading on the feet of my charge while rapidly reading aloud from his tremendous stack of papers.

No sooner would he finish and drop a page than it would, as if guided by a gentle human hand, slowly descend and add itself neatly to the accruing stack on the floor.

What he was reading was nonsense, a fantastical poem or rambling drunken narrative.

The cardinal, he shouted, feeds on bits of plastic piping. In a ballroom filling with mud, chairs squeak in objection. A groggy hippo (What hippo, I wondered, why speak of hippos in this fearful place, at this somber moment?) rolls yellow eyes up at a hunter seeking its ivory canines. A juvenile jaguar creeps forward, dismembers a poodle in a bright pink jacket.

Clearly the fellow was unhinged.

Among our ilk, many were.

(Ours was not an easy road.)

Fish nibbling corpses in a lakeside graveyard, he shouted. A squalling infant borne away on a gray-black mudflow.

Enough, I said. Please.

But he only began reading faster, soon too fast to be understood.

From the house next door came a great cry, as if many individuals all at once had glimpsed something pleasing to them.

This celebratory sound appealed to me very much.

How I longed to be over there instead.

Well, why not?

I was serving no useful purpose here and could serve none until he was gone.

I cast myself out through the wall, looped over the neighboring yard, had a look down.

A wedding.

An evening wedding by torchlight.

I hovered above at that exact breathless moment before the service was to begin. A crowd of two hundred or more sat in chairs organized into rows, flaring torches forming the aisle. The bride, awaiting the first notes of the march, standing beside her father, gave their joined hands a nervous, confirmatory shake, eliciting a ringing of sympathetic laughter from the congregants.

Adorable.

She was a beauty. As for the groom, he was nervous, attentive, awash in an undisguised reverence for his bride, clearly feeling himself the most fortunate of men.

I landed softly among the congregants, finding much that was familiar, even dear:

The impatient flick of a program that one had already read three times.

The *tap tap tap* of one's shoetip against the metal chair just in front but one must immediately stop tapping if the fellow sitting there turned his head even slightly.

The urge one sometimes got, for no reason at all, to scrunch up one's toes inside one's pumps.

The sudden cessation, just then, of all talk (all chitchat, all gossip; no more leaning over to say to so-and-so, Wow, what a dress, or, Hat doesn't quite work, or, Can't believe that homely kid grew into such a looker, or, The mom's fresh out of the drunk tank but based on the look of her you'd think she just shot over from the beauty spa).

The wedding march began, played by a string quartet.

Oh gosh, goodness.

This wasn't—this wasn't good for me.

I burst up and into the bedroom of my charge, cheeks aglow with the joy of it all.

Welcome back, the Frenchman said dryly.

The last of his pages had just been read. He leapt down from the bed as if made spry by this discharge of his duty. The towering stack, reconstituted on the floor, ascended up through the ceiling.

Rather than comforting him, he said, I advise you to lead him, as quickly as possible, to contrition, shame, and self-loathing.

Well, thanks for the advice, I said.

Or do nothing, he said. Simply leave. Any comfort you give will only serve to confirm him in his current state of delusion. *C'est exact?* How is it said? You let him off a hook.

Off the hook, I said.

You let him off the hook, he said.

Are you finished? I said curtly. I have no idea what you're even talking about.

I am not, alas, he said. I have failed to make the thing clear. To you, or to him. For all its enormity. I seem— I seem to lack the necessary skill.

His evident frustration touched me.

Ours is not an easy road, I said.

He looked at me. I had not been looked at so intently in quite some time. I felt the warmth rising into my cheeks.

You will see, he said. I will help you see. He is no good. I am off now, to seek a different method. *Une approche alternative.*

He gave a curt bow and burst out through the wall, contorting himself into the balled-up configuration of someone leaping into a pond for relief from the heat.

Only to thrust his head back in again seconds later, tears running down his face.

Honesty compels me to admit, he said. It was also of my doing. I had a hand in the invention of the beast.

What beast? I said.

Quelle horreur! he cried.

And then was gone again.

Reentering the orb of my charge's thoughts, I found him attempting to counteract the unsettling effects of the Frenchman's intrusion by recalling his childhood kitchen and its associated smells:

Lard, iced tea, fried meat, bleach.

In a patch of untended weeds outside the back window lay the familiar burn pile. So many happy moments had been spent at that small homebuilt table, the six of them talking, laughing, playing Nail Your Neighbor for pennies.

He let his mind roam over the pile, imagining certain items that had accumulated there over the course of his childhood: a rimless tire, a rusted length of dog chain, the nicked brim of a baseball cap, the pink arm and head of Minky, beloved doll of his sister Willamina, who had one day, for reasons unknown, torn the thing apart in a rage.

I'm gonna need that sink, handsome, said his mother.

His father was washing up, sleeves rolled back, face red with sun, chaw tin in his back pocket.

My charge was a child then, a dreamy child resting one hand on a familiar kitchen counter of warped, stained plywood.

What would he do with his life?

What did he want to be when he grew up?

Wake up, bub, Father said. Tables don't set themselves.

And why's your mouth hanging open like that, said Mother.

These memories were having the desired effect of driving away that vision of a crazy foreigner dancing on his feet talking nonsense. They stemmed from that period when he'd first realized he'd probably always be the shortest.

Did I look the shortest? he'd asked after his eighth-grade recital.

You looked fine, Mother'd said warily.

But that night from his bed he'd heard them talking.

We might think about some taller shoes, Father said.

Five inches taller? Mother said.

Then there'd come a silence that felt like shared stifled laughter.

He'll grow, Mother said.

Hope so, Father said. Seemed like a third grader'd somehow snuck up there.

Well, Father had since met three governors. Had shaken hands with the great Bob Feller. Mother'd once had coffee with Charlton Heston.

They'd lived bigger lives, those simple Wyoming folks had.

Because of him.

Through his good offices.

He'd sent them to the Holy Land. By way of Paris. Only the best hotels. Cars, tour guides, the whole enchilada.

Suddenly irritated, he sternly, even rudely, addressed an underling. An underling who was soft and admired him. Perry. Why the hell had Perry let that Frenchie in here? Did Perry *cogitate*? Was he capable of using his *noggin*? Could he apply that lump of flesh taking up so much damn space there at the end of his neck to *solve* a thing? Could he at least do that?

Seemed he couldn't.

Well, get out.

Get out, Perry.

Have a think about all I've said to you.

Maybe I'm wrong.

Been wrong before.

Although not very damn often.

Perry, get out.

Send in Lars. Send Marie in. Tell her don't dare bring that goddamn graph back in here. It stinks to high heaven. Communicates zilch. How much did that piece of trash cost me? Remember those folks called *shareholders*? Who trust us with their *money*? That they worked hard to *accumulate*?

His wife woke, rose, checked a bedside monitor, placed a palm on his forehead, and returned to the love seat, pausing to adjust the position of her slippers such that the invisible person was no longer pigeon-toed and was facing not the couch, but the window, as if looking out of it.

I did not understand how the Frenchman's nonsensical ravings could have upset such a serious and confident man.

But they had.

Outwardly my charge remained motionless (on his back, eyes closed, one hand under the covers, the other above), while inwardly (that is, as he imagined himself from within the dream-like state in which his illness had trapped him) he rocked from side to side, as if bound and in distress.

I gently urged him back toward those memories of home (those kitchen smells, the burn pile, those games of Nail Your Neighbor).

He was having none of it.

That dope, what crap, he thought angrily. What did that frog know about it? Had Pierre here ever roustabouted in heat over a hundred under Gleb damn Neeling? Who'd give a guy a stout poke in the ribs with a wrench because some minor safety protocol had been (briefly) neglected? Well, Neeling had been right to do it. He sure had. Safety first. Injuries cost a company. You didn't want to see a fellow injured. So, therefore: firmness. Be a little rough. That way, the lesson got in there.

Net result?

Fewer people hurt.

Neeling was a doer, God love him, the whoring old bastard.

You know one thing you rarely heard about in the good old U.S.A. anymore? Monsieur Frog? A young fellow dying of appendicitis. At twenty-eight. Like Grandpa's brother had. Because a road got washed out. And the horse-drawn cart couldn't make it through. Imagine you go back in time and drop that young guy into the backseat of a big old SUV, fly him over a perfect four-lane to some gleaming modern hospital, save his life.

There was a story often told. Perhaps you've heard this one. Don't stop me if you have, though, ha ha (I dearly love to tell it): Little boy's grousing: doesn't like cars. Because of "the pollution." You know where this one's going, I bet. The father pulls the car over to the side of the road. "Then I suppose you'll want to walk."

End of objections from el kiddo.

Your choice, Jacques.

Dying in the back of a horse cart stuck in the mud? Or zinging toward help, air-con blasting?

Anyone with a lick of sense would choose the latter.

We had.

The world had.

That was what was so damn stupid about it. People forgot the empty larder. Forgot *drought*, forgot *famine*. Forgot what it was like to be at the mercy of the world. The Nesbitts'd brought over a charity basket. During that lean period. After the hay burned up, the little feeder stream went dry, Bremer refused to re-up their loan. You best believe I was drooling. Father shot me a look. Move the slightest muscle toward that basket, my young swain, his eyes were saying, you'll find yourself bunking down in the barn with the heifers.

The bread in that basket was rock-hard and the bacon stringy and the apples home to more than a few worms.

But to us it was a feast.

Whereas nowadays folks padded past climate-controlled cases of out-of-season vegetables and fish from faraway seas and meat from animals who fed in meadows under mountain ranges whose names a person could hardly pronounce, thinking, Yap, yap, yap, big deal, pork from Denmark, salmon from the Bering Strait, loaves of woven bread from Ferrara, all of this is my *right*.

When what it was, was a goddamn *miracle*.

How had that bounty made its way here?

Did it *walk*?

Just *magically appear*?

Go waltz on someone else's feet, Henri.

A wave of pain washed over him, causing his mind to forgo all nonessential activities.

Golly, goddamn, he thought.

It would pass.

It had to. Had to.

Well, it wasn't.

It. Was. Not.

Breathe, I said.

He startled, amazed at how much the voice in his head sounded like the voice of a real woman speaking to him from just a few inches away.

Don't be afraid, I said.

You're with Frenchie, he said.

He was, of course, in a sense, correct.

I allowed him in, yes, I said. As a courtesy. My mistake. I most sincerely apologize. It will not happen again, I assure you.

I said all this in my gentlest voice, which never fails to charm. A charge, frightened, resides alone in the baffling country of their illness. Their separation from the world has begun. They delight in any prospect of an ally. The rest of creation has dimmed. Everything on which they have depended begins crumbling away before their very eyes.

Then I appear.

Get lost, he said angrily. I don't want you.

This was—

Unusual.

To say the least.

Normally I am received quite warmly.

Get thee behind me, he growled. Satan.

In his mind (and only in his mind, for he had not moved or been outwardly conscious for many hours now) he drew back his arm in an awkward, preparing-to-throw-a-karate-chop motion that, in his vital years, he had often directed at underlings who annoyed him beyond a certain limit.

As if intending to strike me (!).

Well, I never.

I launched out through the wall, floated to the ground, stumbled across the drive, past the auto and the fountain of the golden dog.

Because upset, I found myself sinking into the earth to such an extent that soon only the tip of my hairdo was visible, scootering along that asphalt surface, somewhat resembling the fin of a shark.

A solitary nightbird stood in my path, watching as my hairdo tip progressed toward it, perhaps mistaking it for prey, until my fin passed directly through its puffy chest, giving it a fright, sending it up to the lowest branch of an overhanging tree to sit there flustered, wondering what had just happened to it.

Managing gradually to compose myself, I returned to the surface and found myself standing before a redwood fence hung heavily with star jasmine.

From the other side came the sounds of the wedding crowd.

Feeling peevish, I passed through.

The ceremony was over, dinner about to begin.

From across the yard came a smell I associated with (my

goodness) "Jardine's Smorgasbord": a combined smell of "mashed potatoes," "green beans," and "just-baked bread."

Oh, gosh, yes: "Jardine's."

In "Indiana."

Along a wide bend in "Sherwood Ave."

Among that familiar row of "scrawny pines."

Under an awning, two chefs sliced away at massive slabs of beef and ham as a third chef fastidiously adjusted the position of an even larger turkey. On the far side of a three-story glass wall, a stream of children appeared, spilling like a candy-colored waterfall down a stairway inside. Two of their number struggled ineptly with a sliding door until a frail old man joined them in the struggle, pulling the door open just wide enough for the child-stream to exit and flow, with a delighted high-pitched interrogatory babble, over to the turkey-adjusting chef. One little girl now reaching up timidly to touch the turkey, the chef wagged a colorfully sprigged leg at her, and the entire child-stream reversed itself in terror and fled back inside through the narrow door-gap, nearly knocking over the helpful old man, leaving behind one little fellow who ran smack into the glass, then sat on his bottom deciding whether to cry. Deciding against, he rose, felt around as if ascertaining what was glass and what was not, then passed tentatively through the gap, rejoining his cohort, which began screaming with delight that he had, after all, not been taken alive by the evil chef. It was agreed collectively that the thing to do was drop to all fours en masse and slip beneath another long serving table and crawl along the length of it, then pop up again on the far end and hop, hop, hop in place, ecstatic to find that there still existed, as far as they could tell, no limit whatsoever on how loud they could be or where in the party they could go. A source of maraschino cherries being located, an approach soon developed: stand tugging at the trousers or skirts of those adults milling around the source until several cherries at once were handed down wrapped in a napkin.

I found myself getting teary. Like I used to.

At weddings.

It was all so dear:

New dresses, suits, shoes; shiny ties in the torchlight; a man's large hand resting proudly upon the slender back of his date; mingled smells of perfume and cologne; memories arising of other weddings one had attended, of one's own wedding, of weddings one had seen in movie-films; the clacking of plates set down upon tables recently unfolded; a feast spread out on a red-clothed table (the beef, the ham, the turkey; Cornish game hens bundled, browned, sauced; steaming heaps of fried calamari; a color-rich cluster of vegetable dishes; a heap of sliced bread); massive (white, brown, yellow) dollops of custard beckoning from a second, yellow-clothed dessert table; and soon the dancing would begin, the dancers, at first reluctant, made gradually bold by drinks and the sideways smiles of their fellow dancers, this collective feeling arising among them: Well, here we are, folks, together, under the moon, still alive, and though, true enough, we're ruining our new clothes with spilled drinks and sweat, what the hey, use it or lose it, right, kids?

Goodness, I thought.

I was more Jill "Doll" Blaine than I had been in quite some time.

On the other hand: How fun.

I just felt like pulling that bride and groom aside and hugging them and going, Goshdarnit, you kids really seem to love each other and I wish you all the luck in the world, and I hope, I really do hope, that you'll be (I truly mean this) as happy as me and *this one here*, who, though he may not look like much, ha ha, and can sometimes be a real grumpy-puss, I'll tell you what: heart of gold, and you two should be so lucky, and I hope and pray you will be, too, and wind up just as happy as—

As Lloyd and I.

As Lloyd and I had been. Yikes.

Gosh.

Anyways.

That was in the past.

That was not for me. Not anymore.

I had been *elevated*.

A man holding a drink dragged a folding chair to the fence and stepped up on it, trying for a better look over at the home of my charge. *Whisking* to him, I entered the orb of his thoughts. He knew my charge by name and reputation, and part of the reason he had agreed to come to this wedding at all, with his sister, who needed a date, was the proximity of the house of my charge, who he very much admired, being as my charge was a self-made guy and knew what was up and got it about the American dream and was someone this gentleman saw himself as emulating though his own business was on a much more modest scale, consisting, as it did, of (only) three oil-change places.

That is: places one went to get one's oil changed.

Lloyd had been an "absolute fiend" about that.

"Timely oil changes" having been proven to "prolong the life" of the—

No, no, no.

My place was not here, among these revelers, but over there, in the house of the (ugh) dying.

Shame.

Shame on me.

I vaulted up, through the branches of a magnolia, into the bedroom of my charge.

The Frenchman sat in an armchair in one corner, as if awaiting me.

He did not seem the same man. He looked younger, was glowing with good health, was out of his mechanic's garb and wearing the most beautiful set of evening clothes.

Was even twirling a top hat on an ebony cane.

I have found a better method, he said.

He smiled, stood up, lurched toward me with surprising quickness and, before I could step aside, passed into me.

What's happening? I said.

He abided there, taking a deep breath in, then letting it out.

And, of the instant, I was not me but a schoolgirl from Pennsylvania.

The nerve! I felt.

And yet:

She had long red hair, was tall for her age, was intelligent, wrote poetry, could do seven back walkovers in a row; was (I could feel it) lovely, and knew it.

She was thinking, just now (or had been, as he'd sampled her mind) about (of all things) the weather.

Always, for her fourteen long years on this earth, the seasons had passed in a predictable way: the oppressive close damp heat at the end of August made a girl feel like summer was shutting down (as if August were a dear friend who'd just learned he was to be sent away and was pleading with you not to forget the beautiful times you'd spent together during those first precious weeks of him) and then came fall's gradual browning/oranging and, oh, the smell of the covers of one's new notebooks, plus that good old *I am back to learning again among my summer-changed friends* feeling, and maybe, let's say, as you walked to school, a drenching autumn rain converted the leaves underboot into a paint-exuding mush that stained the sidewalk purplish, which, she had to admit, she just *loved* that.

Especially if, for example, in a window of the old Murphree house, on that dull dark rainy morning, a single candle burned.

Which would be spooky.

But in a good way.

Only this year: uh, no, everything was wonky in the extreme all of the sudden. The heat positively *crushed* a gal all through October (Halloween being a big sweatfest because one had chosen to be, duh, a bear) and then more of the same in November, until finally you had to, sadly, bail on the four new sweaters Mom had bought you at Target (sorry, guys, maybe next year) and then came a freaky snow so heavy or even copious it cracked a beam in the roof, or so said Dad, who ought to know, since he spent half his life up there. Which snow was, at least, you know, *seasonal*. Like, festive and all? But then, for two solid days (in December!) August *returned*, and one morning the yard was this total sudden *lake* from all the melting snow, and the swing set tipped all the way over on its own for no reason whatsoever just because something underground had fritzed out or whatnot from all the melting (!).

Then, a week later, as you were helping Mom get the Christmas tree in (because that's the kind of super-thoughtful kid you were, ha ha, but seriously), both of you just *pouring off* sweat, because it was like *eighty* or something, you started back for the new tree stand in the trunk only to find hundreds of hailstones zipping down like little *lunch boxes* or whatnot, and you and Mom had to wait on the porch for the utter madness out there to abate (meaning "stop") or else get good and brained, which, meanwhile, smaller hailstones kept plunking down and bouncing back up out of the trunk as if the trunk were not a trunk at all but a gosh-darned trampoline, didn't it seem that way? Mom said.

And she had to admit, yes, exactly, spot-on observation, Mom.

The Frenchman stepped abruptly out of me.

And I was suddenly no longer that girl.

How I missed her, missed being her, missed knowing I was lovely, missed looking forward to high school, where, I felt sure, I would do great and make just a ton of new friends.

The Frenchman looked at me with alarm.

That? he said. That is what you take away? From this *expérience extraordinaire*? That I have provided you? That she is lovely? That she will have friends? *Mon Dieu!*

Well, also, I said (trying to somewhat redeem myself in his eyes), something's off with the weather.

Voilà, he said, and cut his eyes down at my charge. Through his words and deeds, he must bear an outsized responsibility.

For the weather? I said.

However, honesty compels me to admit, he said. It was also of my doing. I had a hand in the invention of the beast.

So you've said, I said.

Quelle horreur! he cried.

So you've said, I said.

Do not mock me, he said. My shame is well-founded. See for yourself.

He skim-popped me lightly across the head with the palm of his hand.

And just like that, I was him, briefly, the Frenchman, in a mechanic's jumper, crouching before some sort of metal contraption in a squalid barn smelling of cow dung and gasoline. With a bang the thing went off. From one end protruded a metal claw, which suddenly started turning. Oily smoke from the contraption poured forth from the barn, drifting over a nearby meadow lush with wildflowers, where I would sometimes go to sit against a boulder while working through a particularly difficult engineering problem.

I had done it.

Triomphe, I had done it!

Wait, I said. You invented the *engine*?

To my shame, yes, he said.

Well, I beg to differ, I said.

For me? Former me? Jill "Doll" Blaine? My auto, my car? My "lime-green" Chevelle? In those bygone days? In "Stanley, Indiana"? Had been a source of such happiness. To get in it, when it was new, a gift from "Dad," and drive around town, and have the other kids notice, and wave? At me? Former big nobody? To cruise, on a Friday night, down Pope Street, in that wonderful new-car smell, and join the long line of other gleaming cars, all filled with kids from school, and park at the Aurora for Cokes, then slowly cruise back out, to wave at and flirt with boys who, at school, in real life, I would never even have dreamed of speaking to?

And he, the Frenchman, had played a part in that?

In making thousands, maybe millions, of young teens happy?

Not to mention: family vacations, ambulances, trucks delivering all sorts of wonderful things to people all over town who needed them?

You don't understand, he said.

I'm afraid I don't, I said.

It poisons, *madame,* he said. I did not know it then. But I know it now. I have been corrected. As *he* must be. And you? You are here to *help.* To help *me.* Help me correct him. Which you will do. Make no mistake.

He was scaring me a little, to be honest.

And what did he think I was going to be able to do about it, anyway?

Lie on top of him, he said.

I beg your pardon? I said.

Lie on top of him, he said. Let yourself sink in. Enter him, show him. Show him what I have shown you. That girl, her feelings, the weather. Then I will leave you to your work. If, that is, you still wish to do it.

My charge's legs were swollen, his breath terrible, his color bad, his features painted with the early signs of encroaching death, the lips beginning, already, to arrange themselves into the death-sneer.

Why don't *you* do it? I said.

I no longer have it! the Frenchman cried. I gave it to you. Besides, he has an aversion to me. And is therefore unlikely to receive from me. Do it. Do it now. Lie on top of him. Sink in. Breathe in, breathe out. Then abide there for, perhaps, another full minute. Just to be sure. Come now: no more delays.

Always, in the bygone days, men would tell me with great certainty what I should do and then, if I hesitated, would tell me again, towering over me, smelling of cigars and mouthwash, superior smirks creeping over their huge-pored faces, and then I would, often, nearly always—well, I would *do* it. I would do whatever that man had asked me to do, within reason, seeing this as a form of kindness on my part, so as to not force the poor fellow, who no doubt had a lot on his mind, to, uh, raise his voice or otherwise become, well, frustrated.

Frustrated with me.

The Frenchman was frowning.

It was always their disappointment that got me.

Even more so than their anger.

I suggested that, rather than entering him, I might, perhaps, hold my forearms above the torso of my charge? Like so? Then briefly dip them in?

I demonstrated, stopping just short of entry.

No, no, lie on top of him, he said. Enter him. Don't be obtuse. Trust me. It will be more powerful that way. He will be more apt to receive.

Well, I was not the passive woman I had once been.

I had been *elevated*, was stronger now, could do what *I* thought best.

I'll try it my way, thanks, I said, and thrust my forearms in.

At which the Frenchman let out a terrible groan.

Idiote! he shouted.

But I could tell, by a certain sensation at the base of my skull and the look that passed over my charge's face, that, yes, he saw.

Somewhat dimly, somewhat partially.

But he saw.

Saw the Pennsylvania girl.

My God, woman! the Frenchman shouted. I *gave* that to you. Do you not see? I no longer *have* it. Here within me. To give.

Nor do you have it within you. *Quel désastre!* You have wasted it! Look: he barely felt it. You have no idea what you have done. *Quel imbécile!* What an excellent chance you have tonight forfeited!

Well, let's see, I said. Let's at least wait and—

His natty suit was suddenly a dull gray and the hat on his cane was no longer spinning.

It was not easy, he said. Extracting that. Bringing it back here.

I'm sure, I said.

Pennsylvania is far, he said.

Must have been very tiring, I said.

And I did it with such admirable quickness, he added sadly.

Then began to visibly age, while regarding me with a withering look of reproach.

As he aged, he shrank, became bent and thin, rotated in space, was soon lying horizontally and, in that position, passed away.

Then manifested as he actually was, now, back in that former realm: a thin layer of dried bonedust in what remained of a rotted coffin in an obscure quarter of a Parisian graveyard.

I will do my best to return, a voice said from within the layer.

Then the coffin vanished, a ripple ran through the now-floating layer of bonedust, which retracted sharply into a single mote, and then even that much of him was gone.

Adieu, I said, perhaps rather small-mindedly.

Did this glimpse of his true state, as he was now, back in that former realm, put me in mind of my own true state?

Of course.

But I was not bothered. I knew very well where "I" was:

underground, Stanley, Indiana, "Sacred Heart of Mary Cemetery," beneath a willow, fifteen feet from a stone bench upon which "Slurpee cup" rested and had been resting now for the better part of a year, and what: a desiccated brownish-green figure of medium height (length), cleaved in half at approximately the hip-line, left arm disconnected at the shoulder, a fuzz-beard of mold on what was left of its cheekbones, wearing, still, the outfit Lloyd had picked out for me (beige skirt, pale pink blouse, black pumps, my favorite in life, a fact Lloyd had sweetly remembered even in his grief), all of it marked by a disappointingly economical stone reading: J BLAINE, WIFE, 1954–1976, the best Lloyd, an assistant deputy, could afford.

But (joy, joy!) that hideous figure was not *me*, not anymore; nor was I the woman that figure had been when vital, i.e., before her demise, odiously burdened with her stunted diction, her limited view, her nominal ability to comprehend, her constrained love, which she could direct only toward those precious few with whom she had been randomly placed into proximity, i.e., friends, family, husband.

No: *this*, this now, was me: vast, unlimited in the range and delicacy of my voice, unrestrained in love, rapid in apprehension, skillful in motion, capable, equally, of traversing, within a few seconds' time, a mile or ten thousand miles.

The champion of a cause I would never forsake:

To comfort.

To comfort whomever I could, in whatever way I might.

For this was the work our great God in Heaven had given me.

Despite the Frenchman's assertion to the contrary, the mind-sample delivered by my forearm-immersion concerning the lovely girl in Pennsylvania seemed, indeed, to have had some effect on my charge.

He was unhappy and anxious, the fingers on his right hand making rapid infinitesimal typing motions.

Can a fellow get some water around this joint? he said.

Ask, I said.

You again, he said.

Ask aloud, I said. Your wife is just there. You'll need to be loud enough to wake her.

Water, he said.

But again he did not succeed in actually speaking.

I'll die of dry, he said. What a sorry pass. For a man of my caliber.

In a Dumas bar long ago a drunk'd been shoved down and couldn't get up. Just kept calling out from where he lay heaped in a corner, under the punching bag you paid to punch. Man of my caliber, man of my caliber, he'd kept pathetically calling.

What a dope that guy was. He'd quit trying. That was his sin. A person could do anything if he put his mind to it. That drunk'd be lying under that punching bag forever at that rate.

A guy had to fight.

So, you were a fighter, I said.

My charge lay there deciding whether to engage with this figment of his imagination.

Was and am, sister, he said.

Despite his disbelief in my reality his mind reflexively tumbled forth, seeking to demonstrate that he was and always had been a fighter:

At Michigan, freshman year, he'd been taking some guff. About his height. Also, was considered a Wyoming hick. Who, his classmates joked, must play a mean banjo.

He'd felt like packing it in, going home.

Well, here's how that deal'd worked out:

Summer before college, he'd worked in the oil patch. Near Gillette. So, when field camp rolled around after junior year, he knew a thing or two. About the rigs. It could get scary. Some of the fellows got rattled. By the heat, by the noise. They'd turn to him: K.J., am I doing this right? Am I about to get hurt like this? About to get my arm yanked off by that chain right there? I feel like I maybe am.

So from a short little Wyoming hick nobody he'd become a wiry bantam rooster of an expert moving low and fast among his bigger, less-experienced, citified classmates, snapping out brisk orders, which they (who previously, some of them, used to do that condescending thing he hated of ruffling his hair like he was a little boy) now obeyed unquestioningly.

Some dunce would be joking around, doing a comedy routine off the radio, not paying attention, about to get himself sucked into a gearbox, and he'd grab that bozo by the arm and yank him over somewhere safe and hiss a few harsh words into his ear there and give him a brotherly pop on the hard hat. Back in town that night the guy whose bacon he'd saved would buy his beers, by way of thanks.

Suddenly he was cock of the walk.

Like that.

Because he hadn't just flopped down and taken it.

A tank. His wife had once called him that. He rolled right over whatever life put in front of him. He'd worked his way up. Step by step. To the top. Very top. CEO. About as high as a guy could go. If he did say so himself. Hired and fired, restructured whole divisions, traveled the world, befriended senators, advised presidents.

Did that frog have any idea how much motor fuel it took? For the U.S. to have one normal year, like we just now had? One hundred and fifty billion gallons. One. Hundred. Fifty. *Billion*. Try to work your head around that, Pierre. If you can. Get hold of a gas container. Of the type used to gas up a lawnmower. Get hold of *a lot* of them. By the time I'm done, you'll wish you were in the gas-can business. Ha ha. Line 'em up side by side. To get to a hundred fifty billion gallons? That line of cans is going to need to go *around the world*. Wait: not just once, not twice: a *thousand* times. And somebody has to go out there and *find* the stuff. Right? Get it out of the ground, process it, deliver it. Was that easy? It was not. Take it from someone who'd actually *done* it. Otherwise, what? Did the frog want to start *rationing*? Was that the notion? Rationing fuel? Who was going to run that deal? Some vast international bureaucracy? Feel good about that, Jacques? Think that's going to be an efficient process? (Been to the U.N. lately? The post office?) And guess who'd get hurt the most? If the handwringers get their way, brought the whole deal to a halt. The poor. That's who. Those who have the least. What's the tide that lifts all boats? Continual growth. Is continual growth a given?

It. Is. Not.

Any idiot knows that.

So: don't rush off half-cocked. That's all he was saying, all he'd ever said. Let's not leap off a cliff about it. What's the rush? Consider the timeline. Cogitate on the complexity of the overall system. Consider Lao-tzu: "Govern a great nation as you would cook a small fish—don't overdo it." Or, next thing you know, some know-nothing from Washington's in your bedroom, assessing how well you're putting on your socks.

Let's keep researching, keep investigating. Even if the Hysteria Brigade's correct, twenty years isn't going to make a diddly bit of difference.

Weren't these the same jackasses who'd predicted a coming ice age?

Put that in your cheese-smelling pipe and smoke it.

Mon frère.

He was a fighter, yes, goddamn it.

When the going got tough, the tough got going.

And the going was getting tough just now. Yessir. He was sick. Maybe I'd heard about that? Maybe I'd gotten that goddamn memo? He was starting to lose it. He'd started seeing things. Crazy things.

Such as? I said and smiled.

It's hooey, he said.

What is? I said.

That Frenchie is and Walkover Gal is, he said. And you are.

And yet, I said. What color is my blouse?

Pink, he said, wondering at the fact that he knew this.

Pale pink, I said.

Yes, he had to admit.

How odd, he felt: an imaginary woman manifesting so specifically.

What are you then? he said. Ghost?

Oh, dear man, I said. A friend.

A friend, he said.

Of sorts, I said. Here to comfort you. In your hour of need.

Doing a bang-up job so far, he said. You want to comfort me?

Yes, I said.

Keep Frenchie out, he said.

I'll do my best, I said.

But even as I spoke, the Frenchman fell in through the ceiling, so emaciated as to be nearly unrecognizable, all but lost in the familiar pair of mechanic's overalls.

He got up, dusted himself off.

Madame! he said. Tell me: How long does it seem to you? That I've been gone? To me? It seems like five years! *Vraiment!* Five years of toil. Resulting in a tremendous achievement. As you will now see! Let us begin.

Begin what? I said.

In response he performed a stiff, hideous dance of anticipation.

Sweet Christ, my charge whispered.

Steady, I said.

Commençons! the Frenchman shouted.

A bird swooped into the room, a single bird.

It landed on the bedpost at the foot of my charge's bed, let out a bright, summoning call.

More birds arrived, of various species, zipping in through the walls and ceiling until they were positively everywhere: hotfooting it along the mantel; offering rapid-fire bows while perched on the rim of the floor lamp's shade; formed into orderly, phalanx-like rows across the bed (even across the frail body) of my charge.

Hooded warblers, *s'il vous plaît!* the Frenchman called.

A pair of birds crossed the room and landed, one on each of the Frenchman's shoulders.

From beneath the female (yellow and green like the male but lacking his black hood), the Frenchman drew a creamy-white egg, brown-spotted at one end, out of which a new example of the species began to peck its way.

Unprecedented spring heat wave! the Frenchman cried.

The baby bird seemed to wither, made several pathetic attempts to drink a liquid not there, then perished in the Frenchman's cupped palm.

Necklace-throated dayhawk! the Frenchman called.

A bird with an iridescent blue neck ridge left its perch and merrily circled the room.

Catastrophic wildfires during breeding season, three years in a row! said the Frenchman.

Overcome by smoke, the dayhawk dropped to the carpet, bounced, lay still.

Allen's hummingbird! the Frenchman said. Cerulean warbler, purple finch, royal tern, sage thrasher!

A single member of each of these species rose and hovered before us, the Frenchman's intention being, it seemed, that my charge should admire the care with which each had been made: the slight purple arc hidden there among the gray underbelly on this one; the shift, on that one's wings, from flaming orange to the darkest (nearly black) wine red; the jewel-like precision of the gradations on the beak of this fellow, which, if inspected closely, was seen to contain as many as nine distinct colors.

Each is a miracle, the Frenchman said. Brought about by millions of years of change. Unaware of the larger miracle of which it is a part, yet a vital link in what is to come. *Lost forever.* Think upon that dreadful phrase, *monsieur!* And then: repent. It is not difficult. I have done so myself.

He invented the engine, I explained.

Quelle horreur, mumbled the Frenchman.

Christ Almighty, said my charge.

I know you, *mon frère,* the Frenchman said. I *was* you. A partial man, comically incomplete, shortsighted and greedy, living only for today and what might be wrung from it.

Go fuck yourself, my charge shouted. You don't know a goddamned thing about it.

At the sharpness of this rebuke, a female loon (regal, red-eyed, alarmed) exploded out through the wall, giving off a glorious, coyote-like flight yodel.

Lark bunting, the Frenchman gasped, suddenly short of breath. Nashville warbler.

His strength, adversely affected by the apparent failure of this grand effort, began to wane.

Bobolink, he managed to whisper, as if, his depleted energy notwithstanding, he could not bear to omit a single imperiled species.

Defeated, he propelled himself weakly up into the air, ascending rather as a feather falls: by a series of small curves, retrograde motions, momentary mid-flight stalls.

At the ceiling he hesitated.

Weak as he was, the molecules of the plaster presented a formidable obstacle.

The birds rose as one and shoved him up through it.

Hearing my charge's agitated mumbling, his wife came over to adjust his medications, the orb of her thoughts intruding upon mine just long enough for me to anticipate, as she was, the taste of the cup of tea she was about to leave the room to go downstairs to make.

For a moment, the three of us were one.

Or, rather, I was simultaneously one with each of them in turn.

Viv, Vivvy, Momma Lifeforce, Angel, he was thinking.

How he loved her. They'd been a team forever.

Although in truth he hadn't loved it much when she'd wander into one of his business meetings sweetly bringing in iced tea or muffins. They'd had to have a little chat about that. Stern chat. Tears had been shed. By her. By way of saying: Hon, I see your point, I was wrong. Thereafter: no more interruptions. They'd laughed about the whole thing. Later. She'd admitted it: that talk had done her good. Plus, she'd said, now I have an entirely new sympathy for your workers. Then burst into tears. Again.

Well.

Long time ago. Easy enough to regret a thing. Not good to get in the habit. When you regretted, folks pounced. You were weak with regret, they felt it, they pounced.

Then what? You had less power, could do less good.

So: no regrets.

Ever.

He looked so frail, his wife was thinking. When he was weak like this—in a crowd of taller men, nervously twisting a sheaf of papers, feeling his authority undercut by their superior height—that was when she loved him best.

She was going to spare him every bit of pain she could. And that was that.

She adjusted his pain meds up, up, up.

Then left the room and it was just the two of us again.

Your wife seems lovely, I said.

Longing for peace, wishing me gone, awash in the new swell

of the drug, he directed his thoughts to a long-completed project involving a tight, clayey sandstone, considerable extraction costs. His negotiating partner had been an Indonesian. Baya. Baya Ajung. They'd sat in the hotel lobby taking a third meeting. Nice fellow, Baya. Had a strange gait. Was sensitive about it. Would always try to be last to leave the table.

The drug was strong. Too strong. Suddenly the Jakarta evening was full of marching soldiers. Through the window a sergeant blew him a kiss. A kiss somehow menacing. The unit marched off to a pier where all good citizens were to gather. A frightening pier. He and Baya would be late to the frightening pier. Their food had only just arrived. In this culture, it was considered rude not to spend a fortnight writing out words of praise on thin parchment paper, a roll of which had just been brought to their table by their waiter: praise for the meal not yet eaten. Baya rose and rushed away, his gait miraculously normalized, calling back: Now I may leave table whenever I wish!

Outside, the Indonesians had done something clever: remade Jakarta into the Grand-Place. In Belgium. Quite a trick. Good for them. The Jakarta streets, he found unsavory. Unclean. Lacking Western organization. Every building in the Grand-Place, save the husk of one, had been destroyed in a 1600s firebombing. By the French. Goddamned French. What did he have against the French? He'd lately had something against them but he couldn't remember what.

The industrious Belgians had rebuilt the whole thing from scratch.

Lots of history here.

Lots. Of. Dang. History.

The Inquisition had burned a couple fellows alive in this very square.

Also: numerous beheadings. Right here'd stood the decapitation gizmo.

Per Luc, their guide of that morning.

Imagine the millions of folks who'd passed through here. Over the last, say, thousand years. You couldn't. The mind wouldn't hold it. He'd been part of that. The long march of history. Not such a small part, either. No: in a relative sense, he'd been more important than many (most) of those millions of souls. In terms of influence-on-world. He had been, that is, more important to the lives of the people on earth during his time than the vast majority of those dead-and-buried folks had been to theirs. That was just a fact. Even if you included kings. Strange but true: he'd had more actual power than most kings of old. Someone had told him that once and he supposed it was true.

What a thing.

The moon reflected gloriously in the hundreds of melting ancient windows all around. He'd left family and bodyguard behind, wanting to be out in this wonderment alone. Unguarded, free, walking the ancient cobbles, thinking about his place in things.

How'd he done? Mother? Father?

Good.

Pretty darn good, yep, you got that right, folks.

His daughter's voice chimed in from somewhere: What a life you've had, Daddy. You go, buddy.

Julia, Jules. You wouldn't believe the crap I'm being put through tonight, sweet pea.

As far as birds?

There were still birds, there'd always be birds, birds bred like goddamn rats.

Across the Grand-Place, doors flew open in agreement, emitting an uproar he understood to be the ancient sounds of long-ago parties, brawls, and feasts, an unnerving, summed cacophony of grudges and vows and squeals of pleasure in a multitude of regional accents no longer to be heard on this planet. Yes, there would always be birds, the long-dead folks seemed to agree. Thousands of glasses broke at once, and corks popped, and dogs whose legs had been caught beneath moving chairs yelped, and there were sounds of childbirth and hallooing and spirited objection and toasting and sexual congress (from pairs; from grim, voracious groups of three or four; from lonely, hapless self-pleasurers), drunken singing, mournful singing, absent-minded singing, humming, farting, passionate whispering: in short, every sound a human being had ever made here.

Out of those flung-open doors now stepped many old acquaintances. Of his. Good God: many indeed. Drifting toward him through the Belgian dark. Having been made aware that he was here. Each holding an ominous-looking satchel. Hoo boy. Hot dog. Among the friends: Overton, Finley, Henry West, Bryce Philips (dragging along that familiar oxygen tank with the smiley-face decal on it). (With friends like these, who needed enemies? Lord God.) Here was Al Billingsgate, Jerry Kasin, Rory "Red" Randall. Here were Hayes, Brindel, and Riggs from PR, here that gaggle of worthless lawyers from the late-1980s incarnation of Legal, cowering behind their erstwhile leader, Glenn McDougall. Near the end of every briefing, the whole submissive gaggle would always start nonsensically cross-yammering, so as to not appear mere McDougall lackeys.

He'd often made it a point back then to say something disparaging to McDougall, just to take him down a notch.

Some suit, McD.

McD, sign up for a night class. You seem to be getting antiquated.

Why are you right on top of me, McD? You think being closer to me makes you smarter?

Well, it might.

Wouldn't be hard.

Like that.

Good lawyer though, McD. He'd hammered Anson, hammered Manders & Culley, hammered (bankrupted) Elverson Colley, hammered numerous intrusive citizens' groups and wacky, fringe—

At the head of the enemies was a college kid who'd come up to him once after one of his talks. In Chicago, maybe. Smart kid. Articulate lad. Looked like a girl, with all that thick curly hair. His suit jacket had seemed used, or rented, or like a Halloween costume: faded, too large by a size or two, missing its top two buttons. At least he'd bothered to wear one. That showed respect. The kid had taken his watch off and was nervously passing it from hand to hand as he politely posed a series of questions in the rapidly emptying auditorium.

His eyes were positively piercing.

Quickly he got into iffy territory.

So my charge had to shut it down. By walking off in the abrupt, purposely dismissive way he'd developed over many years of telegraphing displeasure to absolute nobodies.

Sir, come on, the kid called after him. That's disrespectful.

Is that even possible? he almost called back. For a man of my caliber to be "disrespectful" to a naïve brat like you, who's done fuck all?

Here in the Grand-Place the enemies, led by that kid, merged with the friends and the whole miffed shebang began closing in on him in a strange halting ghoulish lockstep.

Jesus H. Christ.

This was going to be bad. They'd feared him in life and he'd been able to keep them at bay but this was serious and they must not, they knew, lie, not even a little.

They were about to lower the damn boom.

Are these folks dead or what? he asked nervously.

No, I said. You're making them with your mind.

So, not real, he said.

No, I said.

And you? he said.

Real, I said.

Uh-huh, he said.

His acquaintances paused, taking final preparatory glances down into their ominous satchels so as to be better able to accuse him more precisely and with less mercy.

You made them with your mind, I said. Unmake them the same way.

Immediately, his acquaintances began moving churlishly backward, still in lockstep, retreating into the hulking structures, the ancient doors of which, having accepted them, slammed shut all at once.

And the Grand-Place fell quiet.

I had undone them.

We had.

You're welcome, I said.

Thank you, he said.

Suddenly, I was real. Real to him. There might, after all, he thought, be guides, guardian angels, spooks, phantoms, who, late in the game, showed up to help a guy along.

Tell Viv less drugs, he said.

I can't, I said. You'll have to tell her yourself.

And he tried, but nothing came out.

Maybe lift your arm, I said. Knock over the water glass on the side table.

He tried but nothing doing.

From up on the roof came a feeble Gallic cry.

Will you excuse me? I said.

I shot up through the ceiling and found the Frenchman on the roof, greatly weakened, tucked in against the chimney.

My goodness, I said. Is this as far as you got?

I am trying so hard, he said.

I know you are, I said.

You might be more helpful, he said.

I don't understand what it is you're trying to do, I said.

Perhaps you have gone swimming in a lake, he said.

Yes, I said. And recalled, involuntarily, "Dodd's Lake," Lloyd's big warm legs closed tight around mine, our "boilermakers" on "duck-shaped floatie" between us.

Pleasant, *oui*? he said.

While, back "at camp," above "pup-tent entry," swirls "cut-apart-milk-carton lantern."

As two "cans of beans" cook over "open fire."

"Heinz" brand.

"Heinz" brand camping beans.

You'd put "marshmallow" on "stick."

Hold "stick" over "fire."

Yes, I said. Very pleasant.

Out there, in the sun, he said. All around you, trees. Beneath you, fish. Now: make that lake tiny. Place it in an oven. Heat it. Only a few degrees. The trees, the little trees, go brown. The fish? Things rupture within. And our tiny lake is ruined: white bellies, big stink. I have seen this. In Uzbekistan.

You have seen, in Uzbekistan, a tiny lake, I said. In an oven.

Now is not the time for the joke, he says.

Not the time for joking, I said.

Now is not the time for joking, he said. It is the end of everything, the permanent alteration of all, a cataclysm beyond—

All right, all right, I said.

You are here to "comfort," him, *oui*? he said.

Yes, I said.

To comfort one who remains willfully ignorant of what he has done is to provide no comfort at all, he said. If you truly wish to comfort him, bring him to admit his sin, then repent of it.

Ours is not an easy road.

Made as we are (of mind, fear, regret) we may become unhinged, prone to unhealthy obsessions. Someone in this state should not be encouraged.

I smiled politely, stepped away to the edge of the roof.

Seen through a scrim of summer branches, the bride and groom were at the main table, being urged by the sound of forks against wineglasses to performatively kiss. In a comic spirit, the bride threw herself at him rapaciously, her hand drifting to the back of his head to pull his mouth to hers.

This appeals to you, the Frenchman said.

Well, yes: the neat rows of white-clothed tables, the people delightedly feeding themselves, this young woman coquettishly tossing her thick mane of hair, the ancient lady across from her, as if in response, reflexively adjusting her wig; the string quartet sawing away, the intoning of toasts, the clatter of silverware, the snorting horse-laughter, the yammering, flirting, misunderstanding; the stray fellow, just there, staring off into space as if remembering something wonderful that once happened to him.

It appeals to you too much, he said.

I just like it is all, I said.

A "jet plane" passed overhead.

More poison, he said, and spat.

Everything is poison to you, I said.

It was not always so, he said. In life, I was a happy fellow, often celebrating. A cheer would go up when I arrived at Le Chat de Gouttière. My preferred seat was at the crook of the L of the bar. Then, death.

Yes, I said.

Death, he said.

Yes, I said.

He paused, recalling.

He paused, recalling, for a long time.

Finally, he let out a wet cough that, in the living, would have indicated the beginning of his end. Downstairs my charge coughed identically.

It's not easy, you know, the Frenchman said. I fly around, observe (I must learn all the languages, in order to understand), appear to those of the weakened living who may see me, interview the recently dead, who tend to resist me. I read over people's shoulders in darkened studies, spend decades in musty file rooms.

Sounds very challenging, I said.

But I must do it, he said. It is a step along my path to peace. Or, rather, a step along my path to *eventual* peace. Just as, for you? This "comforting"? Is a step along *your* path. God willing, both of us will, in time, know that blessing.

I am entirely at peace, I said.

He smiled sadly, then blinked twice, as if to change the subject.

Weakened as I am, he said, I find myself in danger of passing into that realm from which no further positive action will ever be possible. Would you mind, *madame*? Terribly?

Mindful of his frailty, I lifted him up and, centralizing my considerable strength, exploded him upward, holding in my heart the intention of sending him back to that distant place to which those of our ilk must return when in need of a fresh beginning.

Up he went.

Merci, he called weakly from already a great distance away.

I dropped through the roof, through the attic, into the room of my charge, and gently reentered the orb of his thoughts.

Outwardly, he lay as before (eyes closed, lips slightly parted, one hand under the covers, the other above) while inwardly he found himself back at his old school. Having just learned what a plebiscite was, his classmates were holding one. On him. On what he'd become, how he'd done. Always there'd been fifteen of them. In the school. Fifteen students. Then little Mag Ebner got run over by a tractor. A tractor driven by her own mother. That made fourteen. Somehow, for the plebiscite, they'd resurrected Mag. And her mother. Who, after killing Mag, had put her head in the oven. She hadn't died then but two years later.

You'd see her out on the porch, spitting blankly into an invisible cup. Now both were alive again, ready to vote. Glory be. That made fifteen. Fifteen voters, excluding him. Plus their teacher, Miss Eva. One by one they stood up, said what they thought of him. In the end, he won: sixteen to zero. Loving him, proud of him, they urged him to go ahead and vote, vote for himself. Which made it seventeen to zero and Miss Eva read aloud from a joint proclamation: No matter how many negative, accusatory signs might be manifesting, he, K. J. Boone, must remember that, against heavy odds, he'd lived an extraordinary life, full of tremendous accomplishment, and had always done his best and, in sum, had done nothing wrong, not a goddamn thing, and was leaving behind no lasting harm, zero, nada, none at all: a world better for having had him in it, period, full stop.

Miss Eva had admired him early, before anyone else, and had never been shy about saying so. Which'd meant the world to him. God bless her. He felt, just now, like being honest with her. He approached her desk.

Yes? she said, warm as ever, the area around her desk smelling, as did the papers she would hand back, of rosewater.

He hadn't thought it up.

He wanted her to know that.

Thought what up, dear? she said.

What was the—what was the word. For the thing he hadn't thought up but one of the Mels had. Or that stooge of one of the Mels. He couldn't remember which of the Mels that guy had been the stooge of.

With the giant hands. When you shook that bastard's hand you felt like a baby shaking hands with a man. But you could easily lay Big Hands low.

Sit over there, you terrifying giant, he'd say. I don't want you over here by me. Sit there, in that corner. You're sneaky, Conrad, you make me nervous, I'm scared you'll nab my wallet. Or pitch me out the window, you horrifying monster.

Conrad, that was it.

Fee, fi, fo, fum, Conrad.

Then big-handed Conrad would meekly slink over to wherever you'd put him.

Always sniffing after a check, that guy.

In one of those huge hands, a check looked like a goddamn postage stamp.

Because Miss Eva was being made by his mind, she knew exactly what he was talking about.

And rose in her fondness to his defense.

That *petition,* you mean, she said.

Petition, he said. Yes.

Oh, it was nice to be known so well.

Well, as far as that goes, Kenneth? she said. For all its faults? That petition was powerful. Wasn't it? A powerful tool. You'd stand onstage there in some packed auditorium and say: Right here, signatures from *seventeen thousand* scientists who don't believe the science here is rock-solid. Wouldn't you?

Yes, he said.

He surely would. He'd hold the thing up dramatically, let it unfurl.

And unfurl.

And unfurl.

Every one of these signatures represents a *scientist,* he'd say. Who worked and studied and mastered his or her field. Who *demurs.* Who respectfully *disagrees.* Think about that, he'd say. And ask yourself: Is it possible we've got some hysteria going on here?

Then from out in that auditorium would come a sound (or, to be more precise, an abrupt diminishment of sound) that indicated: *minds being changed*. Maybe not changed: softened. The sound of just a little bit of doubt sneaking in there. Folks sitting on the fence were suddenly, guess what? Less on the fence. Even the Luddites/pearl clutchers/prophets of doom were given pause. You could feel it in that new quality of quiet.

Seventeen thousand *scientists*?

That got a person's attention.

If later someone pointed out in the local rag that certain of the signatories (i.e., Bugs Bunny/Mozart/Abe Lincoln et al.) were not, strictly speaking, living scientists: no matter. Not every person who'd been in that crowd would see the correction.

Boom: a win.

And, well, yes, guilty as charged: even after Landon or Lerner or London from Legal had pulled him aside and pointed out the alarming prevalence of spurious signatures in the thing (Thomas Edison? Elvis Presley? Come on, it was actually kind of funny), they'd (he'd) continued, occasionally, to use it. To tout it. To, uh, unfurl it. As needed. The whole thing was a kind of white lie, okay? Like, in an opera, when, to indicate HOUSE, you put up a huge brightly colored cutout of a HOUSE.

Everyone knew it wasn't a real house.

But it sufficed. Did the trick.

Served the cause.

Is that your confession, Kenneth? Miss Eva said.

Yes, he said, relieved to have it off his chest.

Her eyes narrowed the way they would when a student needed a correction and she was about to give it.

I don't envy you, Kenneth, she said. Even with all your many houses.

Miss Eva had always lived in a modest house by the fairgrounds. And often spoke of it bitterly to the class. Her pantry was insufficient. The flour and sugar had to be kept on top of the stove, so, when cooking, she had to relocate these to the dining table, which itself was barely large enough to accommodate two decent-sized platters, which made it all but impossible to host a proper gathering.

Do you find it honorable, Kenneth? Miss Eva said. To confess only the most minor of your sins?

Thinking of her inadequate little house had apparently put Miss Eva into a snit.

Sins, my ass.

Look, he said.

You look, she said.

Something funny was happening out the schoolhouse window.

And don't look away, she said.

Crow Creek was just pure shit, flowing past. A fisherman in hip waders was midstream, fishing away, holding his nose. The clouds had a sulfur taint and the flowers the class had planted near the fence were in flames. The town's dogs raced by in a pack, seeking a source of clean water. The leaves on the trees were turning to shit and dropping. *Plop, plop, plop.* A shit-leaf plopped right into Mother's best purse. What was Mother's best purse doing out here at the schoolhouse? She'd had only that one, long as he'd known her. Later, when she was already old, he'd bought her three new ones in Paris: Hermès, Gucci, Prada. She'd never had any use for them. Too fancy, too badly designed. There was no place to actually *put* anything. Only her old purse would do. Now here it was, filling up with shit-leaves. Mother was going to hit the ceiling. Here was Mother now.

Standing beside Miss Eva. Eek, hello, Mother. She glowered at him more fiercely than she'd ever glowered at him in life.

And she'd glowered at him pretty fiercely in life.

What have you got yourself into, Kenneth? she said harshly.

He's lying to beat the band, said Miss Eva. Lying right to my face.

It's the drugs, he said. You two are. You're the drugs.

It all starts to cave in on him, said Mother.

His long service to his colossal ego begins to undo him, said Miss Eva.

I'll head home, he said.

Don't walk away from me, said Miss Eva.

Don't you dare walk away from your teacher, boy, said Mother.

Disregard us at your peril, said Miss Eva.

I'm making you dumb bunnies with my mind, he said.

Miss Eva and Mother strolled away down a non-shit path that opened up before them, a strip of green grass extending off into infinity, searching for some quiet place where they could sit and disparage him further.

The path was fake too, also made by his mind.

Fuck it.

Fuck this noise.

He knew he was overmedicated even as he stood on the little front porch of the school and observed once again the familiar midafternoon pattern the elm branches made on the dusty burlap mat on which they were required to wipe their feet, once, twice, thrice, once-twice-thrice is nice.

Jesus, getting into the weeds here.

Little help please, Lord.

*

He walked slowly home, observing many things along the way: tire ruts from a specific long-ago rainy afternoon on which Father got the Chevy stuck; a football lost in 1948; the familiar cluster of ancient plow parts near the Robisons' faded red barn. His childhood home was ugly but lovely to him. A warped plank set itself apart from its fellows just there, under the mail slot. The front door made the same old squeak. He moved through the house, noting many long-forgotten things: a chip in the molding they'd always thought resembled Clark Gable in profile; the trouty smell of the under-stairs nook where his fishing gear was kept. Above Mother's dresser: a taped-up inspirational quote from a ladies' magazine, yellowing with age. On the dresser itself: two wristwatches rubber-banded together, a mirrored tray holding a modest array of cosmetics, an owl feather, a ring made of bits of string (a gift from the spirited, unmanageable Willamina). Did the room smell of his mother? It did, it did.

For all the difficulties of his childhood, he cherished the old place still.

One of Mother's slips hung from a doorknob. Mother herself was nowhere to be found. Only the little kitten, Belvedere, long dead, was here, alive again, batting around a paper wad. From this window a fellow could see, down the block, the elegant Minton place. As a teen one night he'd lingered under a lamppost, watching the Mintons move around inside. Mrs. Minton had paused in front of a window, holding up a vase. In her genteel way. For Mr. Minton to admire. Well, that struck a chord. No genteel proffering of vases was happening back at his house. No sir. There it was time for the slaughter. Two goats and a pig, each of which he knew by name. He was damn well meant to help. With the slaughter. Of Emile (goat) and Sally-Bob (pig). While Clarabell (goat) looked on. That night, from her pen, Clarabell sent out a series of mourning bleats. He'd badly wanted to go to her.

Sit, Father had growled. Sit, you.

Oh, those days, those brutal days.

(Dear man.

My charge wanted me to *know* him. To understand who he was, what he'd done.)

Then (a ray of hope) his first-ever time on the course out at Cheyenne C.C.: the lush deep grass, the expensive leather bags, the clubs themselves (gleaming, weaponlike), the way the men (local Wyoming clodhopper big shots he'd long since outclassed) would step grandly out of fine golf carts (like spaceships in their newness) and survey things casually, then issue some offhanded order to a kid (him, a caddy trainee, in that pair of khakis Mother'd managed to scrounge up from somewhere and a button-down of Father's she'd heroically altered) and then, end of the round, the guy would slip you a quarter, maybe a half-dollar.

How old are you, son? Twelve? Really? You look younger. You did fine with that bag, though. You surely did. It's about as big as you are, slick. You two were wrassling, weren't you? Sometimes it was winning and sometimes you were.

It felt like a secret society a kid might someday join. He (even he) might someday become a man who tipped big and padded off across that lush fairway like a king, talking about the best steak joints in Los Angeles/Reno/Canada, about some fellow some other fellows had beaten the living shit out of, after which there was going to be no more trouble on that front, believe you me. Leaning into one another to whisper brutal, necessary secrets, cigarettes held out behind them, out of the circle, and then, once the secret had been shared, the men would step abruptly back, breaking the huddle, and take deep, punctuating drags, as if to cleanse by smoke the sin of the secret, and one of them might cast a glance over at him, the lowly caddy, as if to say: If you heard that, son, I trust you'll keep your royal trap shut.

And he would.

He always would. That's what powerful men did. Stayed quiet. Held secrets. Ran things from inside a tight protective circle, making perilous decisions only they were savvy enough to make, leaving normal morality to the mere earthlings, who lived and ate and died dully down below, never knowing the extent to which they were being shielded by a beneficent distant pulling of strings.

Going home, after a day like that? Heartbreaking. Everything back at home was so mean, so old-fashioned, so frugal. He was using too much dish soap? Having had his morning of fun, he could come down to earth and put every last cent of his tip money there in the Common Jar and get cracking on some badly neglected chores, mister, and darn well stop playing the dandy?

No.

No, no.

It was all too small.

(Did I see? Did that make sense?

Yes, I said.)

He wasn't going to live like that.

So: college in Michigan and that summer he'd become a wiry bantam rooster of an expert moving low and fast among his citified classmates and the following magical autumn when, by way of certain compliments, nicknames, and fellowships bestowed upon him by faculty, it became clear that the mastery of a short list of subjects (econ, sedimentology, organic chemistry) could make his dream (of stepping out of a spaceship-like cart into a circle of adoring caddies who'd just been enviously/fearfully discussing him and his beautiful new shoes) come true.

And it had all been accomplished. Not *easily*, but *smoothly*. With work, hard work, but no real struggle. Up, up, up he went. (Could I even begin to imagine the thrill of that?) He loved the work and believed in it. (He loved the work and it loved him back, he always said.) He became part of a tribe, a tribe of brothers (and some sisters, yes, even back then) and soon emerged as a leader of that tribe. He'd loved the tribe. Loved it dearly. Was proud to be part of it, thrilled to be giving his days to it and to find himself rising up effortlessly within it.

And never along the way had there been a moment of hesitation or doubt or anything but a growing gratitude that he'd been formed in such a way that his natural strengths were just what the world required.

Then came a challenge. A drumbeat, a steady drumbeat. Of objection. To who he was, to what the tribe was about. Their enemies were hyperbolic, hysterical, irrational, over-the-top, panic-stricken. Piss and moan, piss and moan was all they knew how to do. They were losers, trivial people, reckless in speech and action. They took but knew not from whence the bounty flowed. They were rude, dismissive, sent insulting letters to his home, talked him down in public, all while understanding not the first damn thing about what he, what they (the tribe), actually *did:* how bold it was, how risky, how often they failed, losing, sometimes, millions in the trying.

Terrible, I said.

And to come to the point: What had he ever "denied"? Nothing. He'd challenged, sure, he'd asked for a higher level of certainty, he'd pulled at loose threads in certain specious arguments, he'd pointed out the existence of a range of valid scientific opinions out there re what, exactly, was happening.

And for that, he'd become the villain of the piece, the principal baddie.

That must have been difficult, I said.

Yes, he said. Yes it was. Thank you. For understanding that.

But it didn't matter. The tribe saw him clearly. The tribe knew what was what. The tribe was made, to a person, of honest, straightforward, trustworthy, hardworking folks.

Salt of the earth.

Good people all.

He wanted me to know that.

There'd been no sin involved in any of it, none at all.

Then his eyes widened at a sound from across the room.

He was dying, for reasons unclear, in the least appealing room of his magnificent home.

A pair of red velvet drapes hung on the eastern wall, as if to frame a view out a window. But there was no window. The space would also have been ideal for a valued painting. But there was no painting and no indication that one had ever hung there.

These purposeless drapes seemed part of some abandoned attempt to render the room regal. Above the fireplace hung the helmet from a suit of armor. On a side table near the love seat a set of miniature brass knights was arranged around a lamp as if laying siege to it. This aspiration to regality competed with an earlier attempt at an Old West theme: on the wall above the dresser hung an arrangement of antlers, an old saddle, two Colt .45s in an African blackwood display case. An empty medical bed took up what was left of the room but the speed with which my charge's illness had overtaken him meant that he'd never felt well enough to be transferred to it.

Hear that? he said.

Yes, I said.

We were hearing the thrashing sound one of our ilk will sometimes make as it struggles itself into being. One must want desperately to appear and, even so, might only partly succeed: one might arrive in waves, or in a diminished state. One's appearance might be distorted by detritus from one's psyche or the manner of one's passing. Even having succeeded, one might fade away before one's desires were fully realized.

Two men of our ilk, approximately a third the size of real men, stepped out from behind the useless drapes, one from the right, the other from the left. Growing ever more full-sized as they came, they crept toward my charge, clad in shiny blue (three-piece, wide-lapeled) business suits over which, for reasons unknown, white lab coats had been thrown. Then, in the next instant, the white lab coats would be on the inside, with the shiny blue business suits outside, these transitions occurring every second or so.

Gentlemen, I said. You're intruding.

We're not, said the first man.

We're more than welcome here, said the other.

More welcome than you, said the first.

Than you are, said the other.

Than you'll ever be, said the first.

Old friends, said the other.

Of your charge, said the first.

Work colleagues, said the other. From way back.

Mel, said the first, by way of introduction.

Also Mel, said the other.

In life we were both named Mel, said the first.

And both worked closely with your charge, said the other. But never actually met each other. That's what was so funny about it.

Mel G., said the first. Call me Mel. Or just "G."

Mel R., said the other. "R." is fine.

They stepped around me, one on either side, to directly address my charge.

How's it hanging, pal? said G.

It's us, buddy, said R.

Who have gone on before, said G.

To rest eternal, said R.

Though in neither case did you attend, said G.

Or flowers, said R.

Not to worry, said G. We exist in a realm beyond such petty concerns.

What matters to us, said R. Is all the good work we three did together.

In the name of science, said G.

And they let loose a peal of hellish cackling laughter.

Is it lying when one knows how one wants things to turn out and then says what is needed to achieve that result? said R.

Lying when a person uses his considerable reputation and his mastery of public communication to thrash his opponents by redirecting the attention of the general populace, thus infecting the people with the tiniest sliver of doubt, which, widely propagated, becomes a sizable wedge of doubt? said G.

Doesn't every idea, said R., even those judged by some standards to be fallacious or those which have been disproven outright, deserve to be honored with the public's attention?

Doesn't the public have the right to know? said G.

And decide for itself? said R.

Are you calling the public stupid? said G.

Do you not believe in democracy? said R.

R. turned to me.

We were, in life, eminent scientists, he said.

We practically won World War II, said G. If that's not overstating it.

It's not, said R. I'd say you're *understating* it. Because why?

Atomic bomb, said G.

Pretty big deal, said R.

The biggest, said G.

Ka-boom, said R.

War over, said G.

Democracy wins, said R.

Hence our stellar reputations, said G.

Having done our part to save the world, we widened our gaze, said R.

Broadened our stances, said G.

Filled our coffers, said R.

Created a more inclusive national debate on several vital issues, said G.

Stirred up the shit, said R.

Profited, said G.

Insanely, said R.

Allowed dissenting voices into the mix, said G.

Slowed a nebulous debate to a veritable crawl, said R.

Anyway, said G.

Any-old-hoo, said R.

Just dropping by to say thanks, said G.

To our friend K.J., said R.

For the funding, said G.

Thanks for the funding, K.J., said R.

The surreptitious, secretive funding, said G.

Which dared not speak its name, said R.

Utilized, by us, to fund a plethora of press releases, news articles, and symposia, said G.

As well as a number of energy-related think tanks, said R.

"The Council for a Sensible Environment," said G.

"The Intelligent Energy Consortium," said R.

"The Healthy Earth Alliance," said G.

That was a good one, said R.

Again, the hellish laughter, this time accompanied by the sound of the two of them rather mechanically slapping their knees.

Awash in your generous funding, K.J., said G., now and then one of our think tanks might spawn a new think tank.

Even as he spoke, a tiny man, in the exact image of G., plopped out of the rear of G., then sat disoriented on the floor, rubbing its eyes.

Jeez, look at that, said R. You spawned that little guy right out.

Didn't even hurt, said G. Much.

The tiny G. began to grow, and the more he grew, the more identical he became to the original G., until the two were perfectly indistinguishable and even the rate at which their business suits kept giving way to the lab coats and vice versa became synchronous, giving off, each time, a faint *whoosh*.

Friends, said the formerly tiny, now full-sized G.

Of your charge, said a tiny man identical to R., just then dropping out of R.'s rear.

Look, now I'm doing it, said R.

Work colleagues, said the R. replica. From way back.

Replicas of the replicas began dropping from the rears of the initial replicas and these secondary replicas grew full-sized and began dropping out tertiary replicas, who also grew, until the room was so packed with full-sized versions of the original G. and R., all talking at once, that several of the replicas were nudged out through the wall and, while still in the process of introducing themselves, tumbled down into the yard below.

Quiet, gentlemen, please! shouted the original R. (or at least I believed him to be the original, based on the fact that he was the R. standing closest to my charge's head).

The room fell silent but for a few last-minute suit-to-lab-coat transitional *whoosh*es.

We, your dear friends, have left that barren stage called Life, said the original R. And frankly, K.J., from the smell in here and how weirdly stiff you appear, it seems that you too will soon be joining our club, amigo.

The club of the sudden odor of roses, said the original G.

The club of the *clunk-clunk-clunk* as one is dropped into the good old death-hole from which one never bounces cheerfully out, said R.

The black crepe club, said G. The swelling-feet-in-forever-shoes club; the I've-got-just-a-ton-of-dirt-weighing-down-on-me club; the club of those gradually becoming forgotten by those still alive above; the club of those whose every left-behind photograph betrays, by way of the comically ancient outfit one is wearing, one's total obsolescence.

In response to this ghastly litany, all of them, originals and copies alike, began nervously shifting around, emitting strange moans of dread.

But on the bright side, said G.

We want you to know, dear friend, R. said, that we're here for you. Stand strong against your enemies, even in these, your final hours.

Yield not an inch, said G.

Don't give the bastards the pleasure, said R. You are poised to make a clean escape.

Whatever "lies" they claim you told or "harm" they claim you did, said G. Fuck those naysayers! You're about to get away unscathed, pal.

You, like us, were never proven wrong or publicly disgraced or forced to apologize, said R. And, like us, lived well even until the end, king of your domain, eating regally, traveling widely, praised by many, and never did you recant, cower, waffle, or feel a need to reposition and/or prostrate yourself.

K.J., pal, dear boy: *salud!* said G. You really helped us promulgate.

Our views, said R.

Helped us win the day, said G.

And now look, said R. We have won the fight.

The day is ours, said G.

All these years later, and nothing much has been done, said R.

About it, said G.

Thanks to you, said R.

And us, said G.

Mostly you, said R. Let the record show: it was mostly you.

Clambering up, G. assumed a feral squatting position atop my charge's chest.

Don't give in, pal, he hissed down at my charge. Though the seas may rise and the mountains turn to mud and subsume the farms and the forests burn and entire prairies be denuded and through sleeping cities race the very flames of Hell—

You didn't do it, said R., scrambling up adeptly onto the shoulders of his ferally squatting friend.

You did not do it, said G.

And even if, it turns out, you did do it? said R. Or contributed to it disproportionally? By pointedly refusing to use your considerable power to, even in the slightest way, acknowledge, stop, or slightly slow it—

Admit no wrongdoing, said G.

Nobody can touch you, said R. Unless you recant. The world's still out there, filled with our enemies, bitching as usual. Let them flail! You stand at the threshold of the next world, dear friend, victorious and unrebuked.

Leap, said G.

Leap across, intoned all the replicas at once.

If you, in fact, altered the world, the physical world? said R.

So be it, said G.

Who doesn't? said R.

All is illusion, said G.

Leave with thy victory intact, said R.

The two original Mels situated themselves in the middle of the room, threw back their heads, spread their arms wide, and the replicas shrank down and each scurried back up into the respective rear of its original until only the two original Mels remained, wincing somewhat at the discomfort associated with the ongoing, continual rear reentry of their miniature selves.

You two were never welcome here, my charge said. You're not welcome here now.

True, said R.

Hurtful, said G.

Yet look, said R. Here we are.

In the very bedroom of your dying, said G.

The two men bowed formally, G. inadvertently expelling, as he bowed, a final replica just then reentering his rear, which plopped to the floor, then doggedly began ascending that same leg again.

We'll be waiting, said G.

In the bushes, said R.

Near the redwood fence, said G.

To collect you, said R.

Slavering, fast-breathing, said G.

Discussing with relish the good old days, said R.

And the good days yet to come, said G. With you at our side, K.J.

As we roam the earth, encouraging former compatriots in their final moments, said R.

As we hope we have encouraged you tonight, said G.

Each letting out a small yelp of torment, they savagely hurled themselves through a closet door nearby as if to avenge themselves upon it.

Rushing over, throwing open the door, I found only a set of dusty dumbbells and, on a wooden hanger, a green bathrobe, swinging slightly in the backwash of their departure.

My charge's heart was beating in a tumbling, erratic fashion and a sheen of sweat shone on his face.

Sweet Jesus, he said.

Friends of yours? I said.

Barely knew them, he said.

Well, they seemed to know you, I said. My goodness. What did you *do*? Whatever did you *do* to merit a visit like that?

From the wedding came a squeal of shock, as if something unthinkable but delightful had just been revealed to a previously demure matron.

I made them with my mind, yes? he said. Like before. In Belgium.

No, I said.

It's the meds, he said.

It's not, I said.

The matron let out a second, even more shocked squeal, as if to revise her previous, apparently insufficient cry of delight.

Jesus, what was happening? He'd had enough. Of being harassed. Also, the pain was back. Ugh. At a 6, maybe 7. Per the scale Hospice Joan/Jane had taught them. He was all pain now, just about. And nowhere to go. Jesus God. He had to fight back, the way he'd always fought back when assailed by idiots, by letting his anger flow unimpededly outward toward whichever idiot happened to be nearby, thereby unlocking a special pointed creativity that he, when livid, possessed.

He seemed now to be taking my measure.

Why was I pressing him on all this crap, anyway? Did it give me some kind of sick thrill?

Me? I said.

Why not get off him? Couldn't I see he didn't feel great? Anyway, it was dull. A dull topic. Maybe not to me, though. Maybe to me it was interesting. Maybe I was the type of gal who couldn't tell dull from interesting. Maybe I was the type of gal who had a bit of the dullard about her. Was I? A ditz? A moron? A dope?

My eyes (as they had done in that previous realm, when I found myself insulted) filled with tears.

Causing a delicious feeling of sudden power to arise in him.

Airhead, he whispered fiercely.

Space case, dumb bunny.

Then, as if to drive in the knife:

Stupid bitch.

I went into a crouch, leapt up through the ceiling, rose higher and higher through the night air, everything below growing smaller, smaller, more schematic:

Turrets, cupolas, finials, walls of glass, yards, greenhouses, separate shingled studios, sheds, pools, cabanas.

I swooped low, rolled over onto my back.

Because I could.

And because it calmed me.

To be called "stupid"? "Stupid bitch"?

By this undersized, foul-mouthed lout?

Who brought harm to birds?

And associated with hideous, low companions?

No.

No, thank you.

It was sometimes good, when rattled, to think in the highest possible register.

And, by this, preserve one's *elevation*.

So:

The low-hanging midsummer clouds had fled and the canopy of trees overhead resembled a vast mouth in mid-laugh, framing a panorama of twinkling stars that, given the staggering wealth below, seemed to shine upon the neighborhood by compunction, as if hired for the evening to do so.

(Yes.

Better already.)

The streets of his neighborhood below seemed, in their affluence, to be asserting their right to be lazily curved; they lay like tremendous snakes, traceable in the darkness by the irregular contour of ornate carriage lamps, one per spacious lawn.

Beyond the neighborhood lay a forest.

Beyond the forest lay a six-lane avenue.

Along that avenue I went, ten feet or so above it, right down its middle.

The world along it was like the world I had known and yet not like it at all. Some tendency suppressed and kept within decent bounds in my time had been unleashed and any shame about it so intensely rationalized that it no longer occurred to anyone that the swollen ugliness everywhere was a direct result of the heedless indulgence of some pervasive acquisitive hunger.

If I might say it that way.

Greed, greed, one could taste it in the air.

The gas stations were not the simple cubes of my time but garishly lit fortresses of glass, the enormous signs looming over them seeming to quarrel with one another by way of hideous scrolling slogans ("Special Heinek 6-PAC $12 Fri–Mon Lotto-Mondo YES!!!"), the commerce proceeding therein possessing a fierce yet desultory quality, as if all pleasure had been wrung from the exchange, the money below changing hands with a feeling of mutual resentment, as if obtaining it had been too hard on the one side and the need for it too great on the other for any joy to pertain around the transaction.

In a vacant lot, among long reedy grasses, lay an abandoned couch.

I dropped down onto it.

Well.

Never before had I felt such aversion to a charge.

And, in truth, had begun to hate him.

As if drawn there by my presence, two figures of our ilk approached: a handsome black man and a rotund white woman who radiated a likable, perplexed kindness, as if, in life, her tendency to foul up the smallest thing had rendered her perpetually cheerful, placing her somehow permanently beyond humiliation.

He carried a rudimentary rifle and wore an outfit of rugged buckskin and moccasins marked by extensive wear and an almost unimaginable density of skillful stitching. She, in "flip-flops" and an immense, baggy "T-shirt" marked with a star and the words "Dallas Cowboys," was continually and absent-mindedly slapping a bulging wallet against a pair of frayed "cutoffs."

I got hit and killed just *there,* she called out to me cheerfully.

It was "game day," her friend added. Clyda here was making a "chip run." She got distracted, and—

It was a eclipse, Clyda said. I had one of those "viewer thingies."

There were "chips" positively everywhere, said her friend. And Clyda lying motionless there among them.

What's funny, Clyda said, is that the place I'd just been? For the chips? Used to be right here. Little meat market. Manny's.

That also sold chips, her friend added helpfully.

For your part, William, Clyda said. You died in a humble lean-to. Just there.

Near present-day Jiffy Lube, William said.

Brownstone Branch being, at the time of your death, Clyda said, not a proper paved road at all, but a narrow footpath through the woods, used by Comanche and Caddo.

I was making my way east, William said. To Louisiana. Hoping to reunite there with my sister. Suddenly falling ill, encountering the lean-to, I resolved to encamp there for the night.

But you never did leave that lean-to, said Clyda.

Never did, said William sadly.

William was a trapper, said Clyda. One of the best.

And Clyda was "between gigs," he said.

But enough about us, said Clyda.

(But it would not be.

I knew their type:

Tormented, obsessive, grasping, decidedly *not* elevated. Generally to be avoided.

And yet here I was again, as in life: held in place by politeness.)

You did not succeed in viewing the eclipse, said William.

My viewer thingy ended up over there in the weeds, said Clyda.

And is there still, said William. Albeit returned to dust.

You never reached your sister, said Clyda. Your corpse, partly devoured by coyotes, remained rotting in that lean-to, through the long, unseasonably cold winter that followed.

But enough about us, William said.

They turned to me with difficulty, doing their best to feign a modicum of interest.

You, ma'am? said William.

What's your story? said Clyda.

They seemed to be bracing themselves in case I might answer.

No doubt your end was fascinating? said William.

My end? said Clyda. Was fascinating. To me. In my final moments, I was hit by *a second car.* Can you believe it? That's when I knew I was definitely not making it back. To Adrian's. Where my friends were.

Waiting for the chips, said William.

Adrian's house? said Clyda. Gone. There was no house there for a while, then there was this different house. Then that one got torn down. And now?

Forest, said William.

All forest, said Clyda. Jeez Louise.

In the final hours of my suffering, said William, two cowpokes came by, saw that I was of the darker hue, and rode on.

Heartless, said Clyda. Not even a drink of water did they offer.

It was hard, said William. Hard for me.

It's hard for everyone there at the end, said Clyda.

Hard for you too, ma'am, no doubt? said William.

Both were trembling with the effort of trying to avoid once again turning the conversation back to themselves.

To no avail.

Then night came on, William said. And I thought: I shall never see another sunrise. My sister will forever wonder what became of me.

I couldn't believe it, honestly, said Clyda. I actually felt my spine crack. And never did find out who won the game.

She looked at me hopefully, as if I might know.

When Clyda first arrived, William said, I had been here nearly one hundred and fifty years. And alone, always alone.

Alone no more, Clyda said. Am I right?

Alone no more, said William. Truly. What a happy day that was for me.

For me? said Clyda. Not the best.

But now? said William.

No complaints, said Clyda.

And yet, said William.

Sometimes boring, said Clyda.

At first her story completely bored me, said William.

Likewise, said Clyda.

Because it was not *my* story, said William.

Same, said Clyda.

Then, gradually, we learned, said William. We became, with time, nominally more able to endure listening to one another.

And now we hardly mind it at all, said Clyda.

Although, always best to be brisk, said William.

Keep things snappy, said Clyda.

Brevity much preferred, said William.

Get through your deal as fast as you can, said Clyda. So as not to bore William.

So as not to bore Clyda, said William.

(Good God.

Were they *recruiting* me? *Auditioning* me?)

The end is hard, William said.

Hard for everyone, said Clyda.

Hard for you too, ma'am, no doubt? William said, with a prompting nod.

Well, no, actually.

The end had not been hard for me at all.

*

For me, it had just been: sliding into the car, thinking about where to buy the roast (Humbolt's? O'Malia?), then about autumn (did the cold weather cause the leaves to turn or did something chemical happen inside the trees at the same time every year?), putting the key in the ignition, turning the key, and then—

No pain, no fear, just a feeling of disinterested interest as I found myself propelled up through the roof, "I" going off in one direction and what was left of "Jill 'Doll' Blaine" going off in, well, several others.

Then, as if flung by an invisible hand, "I" kept going, across town, tracking Tremaine Avenue, cutting across Elman Park, being guided, it felt, to some specific place, and soon I was nearly there, and found myself zipping through the gray picket fence of a unkempt yard, making a beeline for a grim-looking fellow who sat at a metal table nervously smoking, and then I passed directly into him, coming, in this way, to know rather too much about him.

Over me washed a feeling that no one *got* me, no one *liked* me, I could always tell from the first minute I met someone, by that snot-assed look on his or her face, like, Ugh, no no no, get away from me, dirtbag, pronto.

And that starts to eat at a guy.

You think I'm shit? Okay, you got it, I'm shit.

Watch your wallet, watch your back, watch your house, fuckhead.

Like that.

People were *stupid*, you could mess with them so *easy*. They left their doors open, kept their keys under the mat, loaned you their car, told you around what time the security guard generally dozed off, believed it when you said that your mom recently died, your grandpa had dementia, you yourself had a fast-growing melanoma and used to be in the CIA and still knew some pretty badass hombres over there.

Felt: Best hop up and get rid of the incriminating mess in the basement (auto manuals, tin snips, a plastic bin with a red label reading EXPLOSIVES), plus that extra lump of C-4 in the shed which, no worries, I had a plan, which was what those burlap bags tucked under the back steps were all about. (Mastermind!)

Felt: At peace or something like it for the first time in—well, ever. I'd done it. Had made a plan and seen it through. Unlike my plan to bring a live kangaroo to the U.S. and make it box a bobcat. Or my plan to have a restaurant that served only scrambled eggs.

I'd set out to blow up that pockmarked little shit of a cop who'd put me away once before and meant to do it again, and now that jagweed was—guess what?—blown up.

Check that shit off the list.

Suddenly I knew what had happened, and why:

Ha ha, oh gosh, I realized, I'd been *blown up*.

Blown up by (I suddenly knew his name) Paul Bowman, who'd meant to blow Lloyd up but had blown me up instead, because Lloyd and I had switched cars, just for today, so Lloyd could take mine to the shop.

I tried desperately to ease out of Paul Bowman but found I couldn't.

Whoever/whatever had put me in there wished me to stay put.

Wondering: Had the deed really been done?

If so, with me not going back to jail and all, I could go ahead and have that family I'd always wanted, one that would admire the shit out of me, as in: Thanks, God, for giving us this dude who's so frigging responsible because, even though he could still be out there getting all kinds of tail, instead he scores us this tight little rental, with a garage for all his tools and a ping-pong table out back on which he and the son he'd soon have, off his foxy wife, once he met her, would play a nightly game after dinner, although, however, if I, Paul Bowman, a.k.a. "the Bow," started losing and said it was time for bed? Kid best *jump*.

Daddy, the kid might ask. Did you ever kill a man?

I'd rather not answer that, son. Get out of here. Go clean your room. Or else.

From that, the kid would know that, yeah, it was sometimes necessary to blow a motherfucker up, if that motherfucker started threatening your family.

The family you might someday have.

Wisdom that will serve you well, my son, as you grow into a man, a man always a little scared of your badass dad, as is right and salvatory.

Because I was now Bowman he suddenly did not seem strange to me.

At all.

Who else could he have been but exactly who he was?

He seemed, if I may say it this way, *inevitable.*

An *inevitable occurrence,* upon which, therefore, it would be impossible, even ludicrous, to pass judgment.

He had left his mother's womb with a particular predisposed mind and started living, and immediately that predisposed mind had run up against various *events,* and been altered in exactly the way such a mind, buffeted by those exact events, *would* be altered, and all the while he, Bowman, trapped inside Bowman, had believed he was making choices, but what looked to him like choices had been so severely delimited in advance by the mind, body, and disposition thrust upon him that the whole game amounted to a sort of lavish *jailing.*

His feelings (of rage, of shame, of being worthless, of needing to lash out preemptively at even the slightest threat) were all real and he must suffer them every day, and why? Because he had been born *him.* But he had not *chosen* to be born him. That had just *happened* to him. And then life had happened to that *him,* exerting upon it certain deleterious effects, including, but not limited to, the desire to blow up Lloyd, whom he perceived (correctly, by the way, in the relative sense) to be his enemy.

At what precise moment could Paul Bowman have become other-than-Paul-Bowman?

And how? How was the change, the opting out, the departure from the formed-in-the-womb, the choosing to be other than what one was, supposed to *occur,* precisely?

He had been done badly, by fate, from the beginning, having been born with certain disadvantages (limited intelligence, crude features, an almost nonexistent sense of curiosity), and then, as he grew, had acquired a host of concomitant disadvantages, such as: a strange, aggressive manner of speaking, a predisposition to be offended, regrettable taste in clothing, and a tendency to slip too easily into mindless reactive violence.

But what, of all of the above, could have been changed *by him*?

That is: even his ability to alter/overturn such negative predispositions as existed in him had also been, I saw, predetermined (baked in, as it were). Yes: even *that*—his ability to improve himself by willing himself to do so—was inherent, fixed, non-negotiable, had been granted to/forced upon him at birth.

Likewise his ability to alter his ability to alter his abilities.

Likewise his ability to alter his ability to alter his ability to alter his abilities.

And so on, in perpetual series.

From there inside him, I regarded Bowman, his left leg shaking madly beneath the table.

He was so agitated, so ashamed, so afraid of being caught and also (good Lord) would soon learn that he'd blown up *the wrong person,* a mistake he would then (stupid! stupid!) have to add to the long list of mistakes he'd made, dating back to his earliest days, like, for example, the time he'd drunk a whole little pot of glue in kindergarten because it had looked so much like a thing of real milk.

Imagine a fellow in manacles: hungry, thirsty, flea-bitten, tormented by his mind in hideous ways. And you (unmanacled, free, comfortable, sane) walk past.

You cannot free him.

But you might comfort him.

I felt a new and powerful truth being beamed directly into me, by a vast, beneficent God, in the form of this unyielding directive:

Comfort.

Comfort, for all else is futility.

And I did so: I comforted Bowman as best I could.

I was not very good at comforting back then.

But am extremely good at it now.

Having comforted three hundred and forty-three charges.

To date.

Including my present charge.

Speaking of which.

Good God, what was I doing?

What was I doing *here*, on this filthy couch, so far from where I was needed?

My charge was going through a terrible crisis, the worst of his life. Yes, he was rude, abrupt, condescending, insulting.

But a person could hardly be expected to be his best self under such trying conditions.

I exploded up, Clyda and William seemingly oblivious to my departure.

I got hit and killed just *there*, Clyda called out to no one in particular.

It was "game day," William mumbled. Clyda here was making a "chip run." She got distracted, and—

It was a eclipse, Clyda said sadly. I had one of those "viewer thingies."

I raced back toward the home of my charge, along the avenue, above the woods, regretting the time I'd wasted.

God forbid he'd died in my absence.

Here was his neighborhood, a sprawl of mansions in yards big as parks.

Here was his home, the largest one of all.

I burst in through the bedroom wall, glided down into the orb of his thoughts.

Where'd you go? he said.

Away, I said. To collect myself.

Two fingers on his exposed hand were inscribing an inch-long, stroking arc across the comforter.

Earlier I may have spoken unkindly to you, he said. Called you certain unkind names.

Satan, I said.

Yes, he said.

Bitch, I said.

Yes, he said.

Stupid bitch, I said.

I'm not myself, he said.

You're dying, I said, more bluntly than I might normally have done.

My charge fell silent. His thoughts grew fearful.

It was time.

Time for him to know me.

Attend, I said, commandingly.

My tone snapped him to attention.

You stand accused, I said. Of something. Something involving the weather. You find yourself reluctant to engage with these accusations, lest they invalidate all that you have accomplished.

He gave a small grunt of surprise.

Yet these accusations torment you, I said. They loom large as your time approaches. You fear that you may, at the hour of your death, be dominated by them, sent into a panic, and perish in a state of agitation.

No, he said.

Yes, I said.

A faux–Old West clock on the mantel let out a conspicuous tick, the first it had made all night.

He was off-balance, stung, receptive.

I could now offer him the most precious gift of all.

But be not afraid, I said. For you are *inevitable. An inevitable occurrence.*

Another tick from the clock.

Who else could you have been but exactly who you are? I said. Did you, in the womb, construct yourself? All your life you believed yourself to be making choices, but what looked like choices were so severely delimited in advance by the mind, body, and disposition thrust upon you that the whole game amounted to a sort of lavish *jailing.*

The clock let out two more ticks, then fell silent.

Not following, he said.

What makes the bars of that jail? I said. Your pride in the glories you have accomplished. But if your worth depends on your glories, it must also depend on your sins, which, in your case, are grievous. Are they not? However: forswear the glory, forswear the culpability. The self is the culprit. With the self disavowed, what blame or glory can possibly affix to it?

Not following at all, he said.

Let these ideas enter your heart, I said. And thereby be moved toward *elevation.*

Just then a smell came into the room.

Good smell, mostly. To him. Familiar, anyway: prairie grass at dawn, a little cow shit, strangely sweet, a bonfire burning somewhere, but not for fun. It was a work fire and someone'd dropped in a hunk of molded plastic, maybe. Like that. A tumbleweed blew through and a black calf was nibbling at a cabbage garden near the closet door.

What's this, my charge said.

Not sure, I said.

The bonfire smoke cleared and the calf was startled away by a thrown stone. A human figure suddenly stood at the foot of the bed.

Father, said my charge, amazed.

What are you, his father said, looking around at the spacious, high-ceilinged room. Big dang deal?

My charge nodded shyly.

Best get over it, his father said. Because look where you're at.

True, thought my charge.

He had not seen this coming, this difficult end.

I had a few of 'em, Father said.

What? said my charge.

Sorrowful regrets, said Father. One was, I was too harsh. With you. Was I?

Maybe, he said.

All right, then, Father said. So I was. What to do? You see where I'm headed with this.

No, sir, said my charge.

It was good to see the old man again. In that familiar country slouch. He was missing the index finger of his left hand from the famous threshing accident and always kept that hand in his front jeans pocket. Sometimes he'd take something out of that pocket (a penny, a lint wad, the last bit of a pencil) and squint at it as if it were more deserving of his attention than whatever it was you were saying. If he ever caught you staring at the stub he'd be brusque with you rest of the day.

But he seemed different now: kinder, lighter.

Wouldn't you think this little guy'd be cured by now? he said almost merrily, raising the maimed hand.

Are you real? my charge said. Sir? Or am I making you with my mind?

His father inclined his bony, sunburned head at me.

Ast her, he said.

He'd always done this, said "ast" for "ask."

A fellow could ast around, find out about a thing if he had some get-up-and-go.

My charge had been a bright child and around the age of six this mispronunciation had begun to embarrass him. Once he'd corrected his father in public.

Once.

His father was of our ilk, as was the black calf, who had now drifted back into the room and stood near the love seat, gnawing contentedly on one of its cushions.

Real, I said.

A sweet, pre-crying feeling came over my charge.

All these years, he'd imagined that his father had thought him too short, slow, studious, undisciplined, soft, not man enough.

Now here the old fellow was.

To patch things up.

In his fashion.

Oh, Pa, Dad, Daddy, he thought.

His father dropped to the floor with that beautiful natural grace he'd always had and began running his hand through the long grass there as if combing it.

You afraid? his father said.

Yes, said my charge.

Of? his father said.

There within the orb of my charge's thoughts, I felt the presence of a powerful wall that he felt must be continually maintained between himself and certain complicating admissions.

Admissions easily misunderstood by someone not in the know.

A hick, a yokel, a fellow confined all his miserable life to the merely local.

I did a lot of things, my charge said defensively. Important things. That needed doing.

I know it, said his father.

My charge cast a furtive glance at his father to see what all he knew. Some of it, Father wouldn't like.

Father's polestar being honesty.

An absolute, cornpone honesty. That brooked none of the complexity real accomplishment required.

Hence the failures.

The repeated failures.

Who's this gal? his father said.

Nobody, said my charge. I don't know.

What do you think, lady? his father said to me. Of this here fella?

(I was hesitant to say.

For my loyalty must reside with my charge, always.)

He has done well, I said. Traveled widely. Accomplished much.

What happened at Aarhus? his father said.

I don't know that, said my charge.

But he did. He did know.

I could feel it.

Aarhus, his father said. Explain.

Doesn't ring a bell, my charge said.

His father stopped combing the grass and stood. When he had risen to his full height, he seemed perhaps five or six feet taller than before, his head being slightly bent down by the ceiling, and was wearing finer clothes, and his hair was slicked back and he looked somehow cleaner, as if he had just gotten ready for church.

His country affect fell away, and he glared at his son with the focused intensity of a wronged, wrathful deity.

It frightened even me.

I won't have it, he said. Won't have a liar in my house. You tell it. Tell what you did. Or else.

But my charge was no longer the child who, hearing his father in the living room, would veer away in something like fear and take instead the dining room route into the kitchen. Something arose in him, instilled by the many tense situations from which he'd emerged victorious, the many lawsuits, hallway confrontations, public fights, occasions on which powerful individuals had cowered before him seeking his favor.

Or else?

Some joker was threatening him, K. J. Boone, with *or else*?

Or else what? he said coldly.

And turned his mind deliberately, even cruelly, to that sad Wyoming shack, that failing farm, his parents' poverty in their middle years, the way he'd swooped in, knocked that little dump down, put them up a new house, hired help, got them a driver, had flowers delivered out there every damn week for the rest of their lives, sent them to the Holy Land by way of Paris. (Only the best hotels. Cars, tour guides, the whole enchilada.)

His father, drawn into the orb of my charge's thoughts by a desire to be near his son after these many years of separation, found himself also recalling these things.

And was shamed by them, and subdued.

Shrinking down to his previous size, suddenly self-conscious, wearing again the dusty work clothes in which he'd arrived, holding a cheap straw hat he had not been wearing before, behind the brim of which he was endeavoring to hide his four-fingered hand, he backed out of the room, begging our pardon.

Aarhus, he mumbled timidly as he left.

I felt a jolt of joy run through my charge in response to this perceived victory.

This petty, mean-spirited victory.

It was quite something.

Quite something to have watched a man savage his own father like that.

He was positively on fire now with fresh self-regard.

You know that speech? he said.

No, I said.

Ever read it? he said.

No, I said.

Ever hear about it? he said.

It—it may have been before my time, I said. That is, it may have been after I—

Aarhus, Denmark, he said. Nineteen ninety-seven.

I'd already come here, I said. So.

Come where? he said.

Nowhere, I said.

Where are you? he said. What are you? Who were you? What sort of person?

Nice, I said. Kind of quiet.

But what were you *like*, he said.

Well, that was the sad part.

I didn't really know.

Having only just gotten started.

I don't know about any speech, I said.

But his thoughts were already elsewhere.

Certain memories were moving happily in him: long working evenings in the cold months of a distant year; a delivery boy who, lingering too long in the doorway, had needed to be rebuked; a growing sense between him and some fellow (Dell? Right: Ed Dell) that the thing they were working on together was finally falling into place. Dell was good. Dell was shy, obsequious, a bit in awe of him, sort of a kiss-up, really, but every now and then Dell would rise to the occasion and pop out a line that nicely sidestepped a too-blunt statement of a thing and reworded it in a way that both managed to assuage the concern and slyly debunk it, leaving the audience feeling they were in the hands of someone who, having examined all sides of the thing, had come genially down on the side of keeping the extant system chugging along in the interest of the common good.

Out in the far distance, on those long-ago winter work evenings (across the mesquite grove, past the Western-style split-rail fencing quaintly enclosing the corporate compound), would be downtown Dallas, looking like a miniature toy town over which strings of Christmas lights had been draped. The snowflakes on the Bank of America building were big as cars but you could cover one up with your thumb from out here. Ditto the fifty-foot candy cane hanging down from the sky deck of the Praetorian. Over the course of the evening, he and Dell would slip into what they chummily called "mind meld," passing marked-up pages back and forth, adding this phrase, taking that one out, and then, at one point, Dell would say, "Try," and my charge would stand up and read the thing aloud.

One night Dell nodded, my charge nodded back, and they were done, and that was it: the speech he'd give a week later, at Aarhus, to the ISPP, the International damn Society of Petroleum frigging Professionals.

What an honor. Keynoting that big bear? They didn't ask just anybody to do that. And not just anybody could have knocked it out of the park like he had.

Like they had.

Like he and Dell had.

Good little speech, that.

What a triumph. Jesus Christ. Calls rolled in from all over. Marie had a whiteboard on which she'd tape up the latest clippings, the most special letters of congrats. Imagine that: small-town guy from Bumfuck gives a little seven/eight-page talk, offers a few modest insights, and pretty soon his logic, his examples, are showing up all over the world, altering the path down which the whole shebang—

Could one speech really be that major, have that big an influence?

Well, he only knew what people told him.

Ha.

But yes.

It could.

It had.

To wit:

Not long after, the new administration changed tack, decided to double down on the more traditional, time-tested energy strategy (sensible decision there), withdraw from that Kyoto debacle. The EPA head (bit of a greenie), feeling ignored, resigned in protest. Rory "Red" Randall ("our" lobbyist, sure, but also a damn fine scientist) urged the new administration to shit-can Mick Watson, chair of the (as Red called it) Intergovernmental Panel on Climate Crap. And Watson, perceived to be standing in the way of the more robust approach favored by the vice president (a good friend to this day, by the way), got, guess what? Shit-canned. Two other greenies with hostile agendas, Sprunt and Briley, holdovers from the previous administration, left the IPCC on their own, under pressure, almost as if—now, this was just his interpretation, mind you—the scales had fallen from the eyes of those running the country.

They'd seen the light, reversed course.

And the course had stayed reversed to this very day.

Because of that speech.

Best part? It gave his enemies fits. Threw them into absolute conniptions. Lord, what a hoot. Some Luddite idiot had characterized it as "one of the most irresponsible speeches any American has ever delivered."

Ha.

What a hyperbolic statement.

Those were the kinds of idiots he'd had to constantly be fending off.

As for the folks on his side (the free-market side, the pro-progress side), if they'd found some value in it? Having seen it as a road map, a blueprint, a much-needed, long-overdue bit of pushback to those who preferred to yell *halt* at anyone actually trying to *do* a thing instead of just ignorantly yapping about it? The knee-jerk objectors, the panty twisters, the doom sobbers?

He'd take that.

He was proud of it.

Took cojones to speak a difficult truth.

To wade in against the prevailing tide.

The pain that had tormented him all evening had slightly receded in the face of these happy memories.

That was Aarhus? I said.

I can't believe you never heard of it, he said. Where'd you live? Under a rock? How old were you? When you croaked? A newborn?

Frankness on my part might sometimes encourage a corresponding frankness on the part of my charge.

Twenty-two, I said. Indiana.

Married? he said. Kids?

Yes, I said. No.

What'd you do? he said. For work?

Phone operator, I said. Waitressed a little.

Ever go anywhere? he said. Other than Indiana?

Ohio once, I said. They had the state fair over there.

How? he said. How'd you go?

Drove, I said.

No, how'd you die, dummy, he said.

Got blown up, I said.

Like, exploded? he said. Hoo boy. There's one you don't hear every day. Blown up. In Indiana.

Yes, I said.

By? he said.

Enemy of my husband's, I said. By mistake.

Hold on, he said. You got blown up by mistake? By some enemy of your— He thought he was blowing up hubby and got you instead?

Correct, I said.

I waited for the cruel joke that must be forthcoming.

But his mind had drifted back to Dell.

Because he found me dull.

He'd gotten a strange letter from Dell a few years back. Seemed Dell regretted having been involved with that Aarhus speech. Called it "deceptive, cynical, anti-truth, sly." "Vicious, in its way." Well, that turkey'd had no objections at the time. He'd be there fifteen minutes early, big shit-eating grin on his mug, pencils all sharpened. Goddamned eager beaver. Used to send a Christmas card every year. Always, somewhere on there, he'd have found a place to write "MindMeld." In his weird hippie calligraphy. Dell'd been all-in. At the time. "Even if this theory's correct, twenty years won't make a bit of difference." That was Dell's. "The world has actually, over the last fifteen years, grown colder, not warmer." It was Dell cherry-picked that zinger.

A year or so later, Dell had the nerve to call the house, leave a message. Crazy, rude message. Seemed like he might be having mental issues. He'd always been high-strung. Once he'd told a whole kickoff meeting what it was like to get a coffee high colonic. Advised the whole room to get one asap. Used to wear these weird ties, with cow faces on them. He had, like, six different cow-faced ties. At the time of the call, Dell had been retired for three or four years and had moved to Oregon or some such.

Then here was his voice, on their machine.

Hello, motherfucker, cocksucker! Dell shouted.

Outrageous.

Viv's eyes went so wide.

What was Dell, drunk? On top of being mental?

Bastard, punk, shyster, wielder of bad influence through your loathsome wry charisma! Dell ranted on. I was so puffed up! With pride! How I bragged! At the club! About my proximity! To you! Proud of the many clever concealments, distortions, and misrepresentations we cooked up, as we attempted to craft a "less negative take," to "gain some breathing room for this essential industry we all love" and "push back against the hyperbole" regarding "this whole gosh-darned issue"!

He'd raced across the room, picked up the phone.

What are you doing, Ed? he said, almost tenderly. What do you want?

I want you to go back in time and get someone else to help you write that piece of shit, Dell said.

Well, I'm good, Ed, said my charge. But I'm not that good.

The whole thing makes me sick, Dell said. To think that that's what I did with my life, with my talent.

Your *talent*, my charge thought. Ha. Oh, boy.

We sinned, brother, Dell said. Against the world, against God.

In the face of this hollow sanctimony, my charge felt an urge to twist the knife.

Well, I never could've done it without you, Ed, he said. Truly. That speech was more yours than mine. For sure. One hundred percent.

In response, Dell emitted this pathetic little yelp of—what?

Despair?

Agony?

Butt-hurt?

Then hung up.

So that had been fun.

Sometime later Dell moved down to Mexico, got addicted to something, tried and failed to hang himself.

Sad, I said.

Not sad, he said. Pathetic. A bottom dweller has one bright, shining moment and can't help shit the bed about it.

Lovely, I said.

My charge's wife swept in, set some clean towels on the love seat, went rushing back out again.

The stacked towels toppled off the love seat.

All but one.

The fallen towels landed in a heap of plastic detritus from his various medications, near a set of fresh, folded pajamas, which he now would never wear, and a stack of books he now would never read. Everything in the room was touched with the chaos that disrupted the operating energy of a household at such a time and showed that, all along, the appearance of control had been an illusion.

From somewhere down below came the shrill repetitive shrieking one of our ilk will emit when wishing to attract to themselves another of our ilk for urgent consultation.

A sound it is not within our power to ignore.

I sank through the floor into the kitchen.

The cry was sounding from somewhere below that.

I sank through the kitchen floor into the basement.

The cry was sounding from somewhere below that.

I sank through the foundation into the underlying soil, past a rotted wood beam from an ancient barn, half a wagon wheel, a cluster of three cow skulls, and a writhing closet-sized mass of living worms, which, as I passed, came alive with awareness of my presence.

And there found the source of the cry:

A spindly old woman with a shriveled, apple-like face, in a rocking chair lying on its side, there deep within the earth.

He sent me to ask two things, she said.

Who did? I said.

Spoke foreign, she said.

French? I said.

Coulda been, she said. How about set me up?

I set the chair upright.

That's better, she said. What they done to my cabin? This aren't it.

You're dead, I said.

Think I don't know it? she said. I hurtled over here. Through space. From where I was. From where they put me. In the graveyard, in Arkansas. Was taking my rest there. I'm always on the run but sometimes I go back for a rest. On my grave. But then that foreign feller showed up. Said I should come here and ask you two things. First was: Are you ready?

For what? I said.

How should I know? she said. I'm just an old former weaverlady in a rocker. As you can plainly see. Who died the day the big war ended. And missed every damn parade about it. But I'll tell you a secret. If you lean in. Lean in, girlie.

I leaned in.

All them years, of my marriage to Joe? she said.

And winked, and spread her legs apart, then closed them, then opened them up again.

That's right, she said. Any and all takers. If they was handsome enough, nice enough. Tell the truth, didn't have to even be all that handsome. Just nice. That's why I'm still afoot. Supposed to be looking for Joe, to say sorry. But I ain't. Ain't looking, ain't sorry. So there. So be it. I'm happy enough. With my memories. That mean little ogre, I did him dirty again and again, but he did me dirty again and again. The taking of me by force, I mean. And when he passed? I never came near his stink.

Good Lord, I thought.

Taken by force?

By her own husband?

Got to where he only got me when he made me, she said. And then I started scratching and a-biting.

Lucky me, to have been loved by a man as gentle as Lloyd.

It was cool and dark there below the surface of the earth and dim celebratory sounds drifted down from the wedding, making me vulnerable to certain recollections.

Such as:

Lloyd's "broad hand" on my back, and "alarm" goes off, set to "country station" ("WJJD," our "favorite"), and Lloyd "springs up" all cheerful and "hopping on one foot," gets "pants on" (coins "jingle" in the pockets) and for a moment in the "half-light" stands "shirtless," hair a mess, raring to go, and says aloud, "David Houston," which is: name of the man now singing.

Ack, no.

I must not—

Such as:

April, "Stanley, Indiana," "rental house" of Ada and Todd Sinclair ("real dump" on edge of "FarmHill Estates"), all of us "medium-soused" and the men "cook up" the "bright idea" of slicing up, with "box cutters," the "cardboard crate" from the Sinclairs' "new fridge," to use to "sled" down "mudhill" behind "rental," and after "first run," Lloyd takes "shot of Cuervo" and makes "playful grab" for me, Jill "Doll" Blaine, and honestly? I just drop into his arms and fleck/flick at his ear with my tongue, because, to me? Lloyd being so handsome and all? It was (swear to God) like Christmas morning whenever he'd flirt with me, especially here, in front of this crowd, because of me being a former big nobody and Lloyd being seen, in Stanley, by these popular gals, as this, like, I don't know, big catch or something?

And that was, I gotta tell you, dynamite.

Dy-no-mite.

Oh gosh.

"Dy-no-mite" was, I recalled, "from TV."

TV, goodness, "TV," "television," wow, yes: the bright-colored, balloon-lettered MarcusWelbyBandstandLaugh-In FlipWilsonBobHopeShindig thrill of it all! Ours (our TV, our "set"), in my childhood, sat "just so" on a "cute Asian table" Dad'd brought back "duty-free" from "Manila."

So cool and all.

Hey, hello, the old lady said. You in there?

Yes, I said.

I remembered that second thing I'm to ask, she said.

On Sunday nights: three TV dinners on three TV trays just in time for "Bonanza."

Your old feller dead yet? she said. Up yonder?

No, I said. Still alive.

There you go, missy! she said. That weren't so hard, was it? In that case, that foreign feller'll be here shortly. With a guest in tow. A real doozy. Who'll get the job done. No use them coming if your feller's done kicked it already. Y'all have been serving weak tea. So that foreign fellow said. When what's needed is:

hard whiskey. As he hopes you done figured out by now: this one's a tough nut. Who's gotta get cracked open. Stand back, now. I'm a-going.

The chair began to vibrate and disintegrated beneath her and she was remade into a young woman: lithe, almost liquid, hair hanging down long: a country girl about to hit the town, because Joe, cruel Joe, was gone for a spell, up to Little Rock, and so: happy days.

She dashed up the steps to meet her friends down to the Pines Hotel, they'd be waiting for her under the overhang, as it was supposed to rain like the dickens.

I stood there, far beneath the surface of the earth, recalling Lloyd:

"Tattoo of boat" on one arm.

Slight "touch of gray" on "sideburns" though "not yet thirty."

Girl, careful, I counseled myself.

The more I indulged in such recollections, I knew, the more inclined I would be to indulge in other such recollections, until indulging would come to seem not like indulging at all but, rather, like a simple, joyful return to who I really *was*. Do you know what I mean? A return to the person I had been, the person I was most comfortable being, the person it had always been so natural and easy and (hey, guess what?) fun to be:

Jill "Doll" Blaine.

And we mustn't have that.

Using my arms like a surface-seeking swimmer, I shot up past a severed length of ancient sewer pipe and a bright green sliver of a child's swimming pool from fifty years prior.

And exploded up into the narrow passageway between the jasmine-covered fence and my charge's house.

Here were the Mels, fast asleep in each other's arms.

Ugh, still here, said G., startling awake.

Tired of waiting, said R.

For him, said G.

Who always disrespected us, said R.

Even as he depended upon us, said G.

Pompous ass, said R.

Arrogant prick, said G.

Language, friend, said R. to G. Lady present.

Language, friend, said G. to R. Lady present.

Speaking of which, said R.

Don't you have a roast to cook? G. said to me.

A car to start? said R.

And kaboom? said G.

Body parts fly across the yard? said R.

Of your trashy little duplex? said G.

Which was, in a world full of mansions and villas, said R.

All you two lovebirds ever got? said G.

Poor thing, said R. Briefest of marriage, zero kids, lived in a hovel.

Not even a slight mark on dear old Earth did you leave, said G.

Although, rumor has it, said R. Bun in your oven.

I stepped over, gave R. a kick, a hard kick, then G., harder still, as hard as I could, and then, to even things up, went back and gave R. a supplementary kick.

Oh, but we are *inevitable,* G. said whiningly. *Inevitable occurrences.* Aren't we?

Who else could we have *been* but who we *are*? said R.

So why would you *kick us*? said G.

Why assault us so, when we are *lavishly jailed*? said R.

Nice *elevation,* sis, said G.

You look funny, said R.

Like you've got one foot in the former world, said G.

Like you've been doing too much recalling, said R.

It happens, said G.

Happens even to us, said R.

I sometimes recall my childhood bike, said G.

I sometimes recall *my* childhood bike, said R.

Which one are you now, dear girl? said G.

Jill or not-Jill? said R.

Trending toward Jill, I think, said G.

Merely Jill, said R.

Poor dead, said G.

Plain old, said R.

Oh, shut it, I said.

Anyway, no hard feelings, said R. Go on, shoot back up there, do your thing, hon.

Flail away, said G.

We've got him, said R.

He's ours, said G.

Got him good, said R.

He's pigheaded, said G.

Pigheaded, with an astonishingly limited capacity for self-examination, said R.

Everything you and your French pal have tried? said G.

Has come to naught, said R.

Only hardened his resolve, said G.

Caused him to retrench more energetically, said R.

That's how it is with us, said G.

Our kind, said R.

We doers, said G.

Who accomplish, said R.

Who bend the world to our will, said G.

Bash us, we roll up in an impenetrable ball, said R.

Criticize us, we put our fingers in our ears, said G.

Kick us, we kick back harder, said R.

Speaking of kicking, said G. Earlier, you kicked us.

We have a dim memory of that, said R.

Then they seemed to smell something on the wind.

Uh-oh, said G.

Nearly time, said R.

Hustle back upstairs, girlie, said G.

His wee body teeters at the edge, said R.

Of his mud-black forever-pit, said G.

Soon will come that special thunk made by: inert load, dropping, said R.

After which, devoid of its former vitality, his sad former-person-bearing meatlump will begin to rot, said G.

From the window of my charge's room a light-rectangle, longing for the wedding, landed instead on the redwood fence, where it manifested as a frustrated, malformed polygon.

Up I shot, bent hard to the left, and was in.

In with him again.

My poor doomed charge.

He lay as before, as ever (eyes closed, one hand under the covers, the other above). In his mind he stood at the window of his New York office, thirty-eighth floor, gazing down at an angry mob swirling around below.

How had those morons gotten here, anyway, from all over the country? With their filthy clothes, their swear-word-laced posters, these supposed nature lovers heedlessly trampling thirty grand's worth of planters, berms, and flower beds into a mudfield like something out of goddamn Verdun?

Did they *walk*?

Ride *horses*?

Don't be funny.

I joined him at the window.

Were you down there? he said. That day?

No, I said.

Is Dell down there? he said.

I don't believe so, I said gently.

He thinks poorly of me, he said.

He moved away from the window. And was, strangely, nowhere at all.

Just in some space of great blankness, with me there beside him.

See me? he said.

Yes, I said.

Who am I? he said.

K. J. Boone, I said.

The son of a bitch who destroyed the planet, he said.

Maybe rest a bit, I said.

So say the cretins, he said.

Well, I said.

In a pig's ass, he said.

He turned to me and drew in close, uncomfortably so.

You didn't have to go through any of this, did you? he said. The long death. Lucky you. Just blew right up. Bang: gone.

Lucky me, I said dryly.

There in our shared mental space, he tilted his head.

What? I said.

Your pal's nearby, he said. Frenchie. I can feel him.

You can feel him, I said.

Bringing some new turd up here, he said. Some new dead turd. To spook me.

If he was able to sense the Frenchman's proximity, his end must be very soon indeed.

His father had been here. His mother had been here (albeit only in his mind). When his mother came for real, his time would be short; mother and father would unite, and all would be done.

Have you considered that matter? I said. That matter we discussed?

He seemed to be drawing a blank.

Elevation? I reminded him gently.

Hooey, he said.

At that moment the Frenchman strode in, looking elated and windblown, white rose in the pocket of his glaringly white jacket, wearing white trousers, white leather boots, and a white scarf.

He was almost too radiant to look at.

At last I have found it, he said. The perfect means by which to set this fellow on the path to repentance.

I'm lying right here, you bastard, my charge said.

Greetings, the Frenchman said. Mr. Bhuti, if you please.

In came a gaunt, dark-skinned fellow wearing a beautiful orange silk jacket and a pair of wide, flared pants that appeared Eastern in origin.

I am a recent arrival in that room where no one is content, he said. Do you know it, madam? With its bent-down flowers? And all there is to eat are stale bread crusts?

Strangely, his speech lagged behind the movement of his lips, which seemed to be speaking a different language than the one we were hearing—i.e., his speech was, by some method unknown, being spontaneously translated into English.

You may note that I am wearing the traditional *angrakha* of Churu, in Rajasthan, he said to me.

Talk to the fellow in the bed, not to her, please, said the Frenchman. He is the source of your misery.

Mr. Bhuti turned to face my charge, retaining, even in light of this new information, his gentle mien.

We were, there at the end, extremely irritable, he said. My wife, my mother, and I. We three, who had lived together for many years, never once speaking unkindly to one another, began, there at the end, to speak most unkindly to one another indeed. Also, the skin of our faces became shriveled like the skins of old apples. Also, the color of our urine went from yellow to black as coal. Sounds of suffering came from all over the village. Men fought at the well for the right to lick the bucket.

The Frenchman came to the bed, leaned over my charge.

Aarhus, he hissed. Aarhus is the thread that connects you and this unfortunate.

You talk just buttloads of crap, you know that? said my charge.

A person makes a reckless speech *here*, the Frenchman said. Its fatal consequences are felt *there*.

Sheer buttloads of senseless crap, said my charge.

Millions of dollars are spent propagating a falsehood, said the Frenchman. That falsehood goes out into the world and alters it.

That's quite a stretch, Henri, quite a goddamned stretch, said my charge.

Mr. Bhuti cleared his throat and continued.

It had not rained in over a year, he said. To graze against a metal door was to be burned. Graves could not be dug for the heat. I had not defecated in eleven days. We three sat on the floor, hearts racing, snapping at one another as if possessed. In the last half hour, we seemed, all at once, to shrivel, become skeletal, look identically ghoulish; it would have been difficult to say who was the youngest, who the oldest. One by one, we succumbed. First Mother. Then Charvi. Then me. That is to say, I had to watch as they succumbed.

Quelle horreur! the Frenchman thundered down at my charge. Behold the vile criminal!

I'd eat your ass, Frog! my charge thundered. I'd eat your ass whole, you pathetic, limp-dicked, troublemaking—

You'll eat my ass? the Frenchman said.

For lunch, fucker, said my charge.

He'll eat my ass, the Frenchman said. For lunch. Did you hear that, Mr. Bhuti? Did you hear that, *madame*? Is this something of which a person should be proud? This, in the end, is who we are dealing with: a bully, a ruiner, an unrepentant world-wrecker, a self-centered—

Out in the hallway, my charge's wife was speaking consolingly to someone.

It's all right, dear, she was saying. There's still time. Deep breaths. Cab's best. Quicker. Otherwise you have to take a shuttle. To this, uh, pickup area. A cab's quicker. And quick—quicker's good, baby. At this point.

She stepped back into the bedroom, sat defeatedly on the

love seat. Something seeming to give way in her, she brought a fist to her forehead, and held it there with some force, as if, by the intensity of the pressure, she might reverse time and restore her husband to health.

This earnest indication of love had the effect of causing the three of us to fall silent.

There within the orb of my charge's thoughts, I felt him roll over to face away from us, the way one will turn from one's lover in the midst of a disagreement.

Ah, nous avons échoué, the Frenchman sighed. He remains unmoved.

Damn straight, mumbled my charge.

Mr. Bhuti, the Frenchman said, I am sorry to have brought you so far. And with so little result.

Now I must go back to that room, I suppose, said Mr. Bhuti.

I'm afraid so, said the Frenchman.

May I rest a moment? Mr. Bhuti said and sat on the edge of the bed.

No chairs there, he explained. In that room where no one is content. Where my wife and mother wait, still wait, for even a single sip of water. However, in that room? No water. For us. Therein lies the torment: what one wants, one may not have. For some there is, yes, water. But whatever it is that *they* most desire? Is denied them. One fellow desires his violin. But: no violin. For him. Anyone who does not desire a violin may get one quite easily. One woman wishes to apologize to her son, for some offense: for her, that room is full of telephones that do not work.

Well, here, look, the Frenchman said.

And brought out, from behind his back, a tumbler of chilled water, down the sides of which ran fat beads of moisture.

Mr. Bhuti drank perhaps a third of it, then stopped himself with what seemed an act of tremendous willpower.

May I be permitted to take this with me? he said.

Of course, said the Frenchman.

From behind his back the Frenchman produced a large pitcher with a painted rooster on it.

Take this as well, he said. With my best wishes. For having come all this way.

I know they will be most grateful, said Mr. Bhuti.

He rose and, taking along the tumbler and the pitcher, left the room slowly, so as not to spill a single drop.

A second or two later, however, he stepped back in.

One must do one's best, yes? he said. Having watched one's loved ones suffer so, then being brought face-to-face with the individual alleged to have been a principal cause of that suffering, one must exert oneself to the utmost, I think.

Well, I said.

Yes, he said.

Placing the tumbler and pitcher carefully on the bedside table, Mr. Bhuti climbed up onto the bed, then lowered himself onto, and into, my charge.

Fuck, my charge shouted.

Sir, my dear sir, the Frenchman cried.

As quickly as he'd entered, Mr. Bhuti rolled out of my charge and stumbled away from the bed.

Now he knows, he said. Now he truly knows.

Disoriented from the transfer, he came directly toward me like a careening drunk.

And inadvertently passed through me.

And I knew too.

The shock of it knocked me down. I struggled to the love seat, pulled myself up beside the (oblivious) wife. I had seen Mr. Bhuti's village, yes. But had also grasped that it was not exceptional, not at all; the entire region thereabouts frequently burst into flames, and vast tracts of it, once peopled and prosperous, now stood abandoned, marked by black-burned trees and a web of brackish former rivers from which every trace of life had been extinguished.

And that wasn't all.

Mr. Bhuti, a lawyer, had, before a certain financial reversal, traveled widely all around his country, and his region was far from being the only region so damaged; other regions, damaged in different ways, exhibited different symptoms. It was all there in his mind: a beetle-ruined birch grove in Kalimpong, a flooded Haryana valley in which peaked roofs appeared to the eye as thousands of toy boats; here the ocean had risen to the second floor of the Kolkata library, leaving, when it receded, the books on those two floors rank with mold; at Shivrajpur, three dolphins, disoriented by the unusual heat of the ocean, had grounded themselves during a beach wedding, leaving the guests, including Mr. Bhuti and his wife, Charvi, at a loss as to what to do.

And it wasn't only in his country.

It was happening everywhere.

Mr. Bhuti, that is, seemed to feel that it was happening everywhere.

I found it hard to accept.

And yet, per Mr. Bhuti, it was all true. It all seemed, that is, there in his mind, quite real, and he had even begun to take it somewhat for granted and had, as had many others, begun to make accommodation with it.

Until, that is, it had killed him.

I'm sorry to have upset you, madam, he said.

Picking up the tumbler and pitcher, he left.

Stay out, my charge said. Stay out of me.

Nevertheless I entered the orb of his thoughts.

And found that he was not shocked. At all. By any of it. He knew about it, about all of it. Knew the extent of it, was aware of many examples of it, knew he was often called out for some imagined part he'd supposedly played in it, but he—now, hang on a minute—he just had a bit of a quarrel with the damn logic. There'd always been droughts, yes? Were heat waves a new thing in the world? Some other fellow (ghost, ghoul, whatever) might just as easily have shown up here with a headful of grass-covered hillsides, serene mountain lakes, forests not on fire, unflooded towns, completely dry libraries, meadows teeming with life, thousands of non-dolphin-interrupted weddings, a field of, uh, perfectly great wheat or whatever. Yes? Tonight, here in Dallas, did things seem especially apocalyptic? Or was it just a lovely summer evening? With what sounded like a pretty good party going on next door? No great wailing and gnashing of teeth happening over there, far as he could tell, and in fact, wait, listen: What was that? Just now? They were doing the goddamn Macarena or whatever that crap was called.

Enough, I said.

Without intending to, I rose slightly into the air.

Madame? the Frenchman said.

I rose a little higher, began floating across the floor.

Where are you going? the Frenchman said.

Away, I said. I've had it.

Don't let the door hit you in the ass on the way out, said my charge.

Have a nice death, I said.

And shot out through the wall.

What a refreshment, to be out of that falsity-filled death chamber.

Over at the wedding, the dancing was in full swing.

Using just the right amount of leg-thrust, I propelled myself off the side of the house, over the redwood fence, and then, controlling the rate of my descent via skillful arm-flaps, drifted slowly down, landing gracefully, just so, among a crowd of dancers on a temporary parquet floor, and *whisked* at the speed of light from one guest to the next (two hundred and eleven in all), attempting to drive *him* out of my mind and fill it, instead, with these thousands of vivid, co-arising impressions.

Such as:

This fellow, gazing over at the aunt of the bride? Is Kent.

The aunt of the bride (Jeanie) glances back at him. (Such heat.)

Jeanie, the aunt of the bride, is having an affair.

With Kent, boss of her husband.

Whisking into Walter (Jeanie's cheated-upon husband), I see that he's known about the affair since March, but hasn't let Jeanie know that he knows, because he's afraid she might do something rash, such as leave him before she finally gets tired of/burns out on Kent, that petty tyrant, whose office, even when Kent is not in it, has this weird smell to it that seems to emanate from Kent's chair, which means it ultimately must emanate from Kent's ass/pants.

Leaving Walter, locating/*whisking* into Jeanie (Walter's wife,

Kent's lover), I learn that, yes, of course she's noticed Kent's smell, but doesn't actually mind it, associating it, as she does, with long, sexy afternoons in Kent's office on those days when Kent has sent Walter to Amarillo on business. If things go according to plan, Walter will soon begin traveling perpetually as part of his "promotion" (arranged by Kent) to Amarillo, to Oklahoma City, to Tulsa, to Lincoln, to Iowa City, and then back the same way (Iowa City, Lincoln, Tulsa, Oklahoma City, Amarillo), returning to Dallas only one weekend a month, meaning Kent will (joy, joy!) have her, Jeanie, entirely to himself (and vice versa) for, say, eight weeks out of every nine (!).

She knew it was wrong. Walter was so sweet and kind. It would kill him if he found out.

But he wasn't going to find out.

Unless she told him.

Which she wasn't going to. Until she decided to leave him. In order to dedicate herself wholeheartedly to fucking and being fucked by Kent. Which, she only now realized, she might have to.

Soon, very soon.

Maybe tonight.

This thought sent a shivering, lustful thrill through her (through us).

Oh, life, love, desire, I just couldn't get enough.

I sent my alertness out in every direction.

Were the people here aware at all of the horrible truth Mr. Bhuti had just communicated?

Yes, they were. Many of them knew about it, believed in it. But were carrying on.

It was, after all, a wedding.

Blasting out of Jeanie, I found Carol-Ann, the cheated-upon wife of Kent, sitting alone at a table near the pool, thinking (in response to Joyce, Joyce Jackson, a bright-eyed TV interviewer in her mind, who admired Carol-Ann for living her life in such a fun, optimistic way that gave hope to so many): No, Joyce, it doesn't bother me at all that I've been sitting here alone practically the whole wedding. A modern woman is secure in who she is, and recognizes that her husband, when at a wedding with many of his co-workers, may find it necessary to offer each one of them meaningful face time.

Now, Carol-Ann, says Joyce, checking her notes. I see here that Kent doesn't often bring you to his office events, does he?

No, he does not, Carol-Ann says. And, again, great question and thanks for having me. Opportunities like this really help me spread my message of hope and never getting down about anything.

That is so true and insightful, replies Joyce. You have labored long and hard, it says here, in the pretty boring darn vineyard or orchard or whatnot of being constantly ignored all the time by Kent.

Isn't *that* the truth, says Carol-Ann. And isn't that true of so many women these days?

At which the crowd bursts into applause.

Although, I have to ask, says Joyce. Kent seems, at the moment, kind of sweet on that dumpy little what's-her-name. Doesn't he?

Jeanie? says Carol-Ann.

Yes, Jeanie, says Joyce. See that right there? That look of adoration he just now shot her? And now she's looking back at him with such narrowed sexy eyes. Can you, audience, feel the heat, like I'm feeling it?

The audience could.

The audience really could.

Oh, shut up, Joyce, says Carol-Ann. Isn't it time for a break or something?

Well, as you know, Carol-Ann, Joyce says. We don't take breaks here on this TV station that runs only in your mind.

Oh, Joyce, Shmoyce, there was no Joyce and no TV show and she was just dumb old her at this boring stupid wedding in this big old honker-ass rich-person yard, watching her gross selfish pig of a husband put his boner for Jeanie on total public display.

Which was why she was leaving. Right this minute.

I *whisked* along behind her, staying within the orb of her thoughts as, fighting back tears, she (we) raced away through the crowd, resisting the urge to check to see if Kent had even noticed we were leaving, the big dope, and whether he might, for once, come rushing after us, having finally realized that if someone loved someone as much and in such a self-sacrificing way as we loved him, well, that was it, that was the person you should choose, right?

Oh, how rich, to be in love, humiliated, longing to be taken back, striding along in new, uncomfortable spike heels, wearing, beneath our elegant new Elie Tahari sheath, some simply *beautiful* Fleur du Mal lingerie, in case this might turn out to be the evening Kent finally saw the light, but no, this was not going to be that evening, and now we had to go home and undress in utter despair and put on our big baggy comfortable Winnie-the-Pooh PJs and sob ourselves to sleep even as we considered how to present/rationalize this unprecedented bailing-on-the-wedding business in the most positive light possible when Kent came home.

If, in fact, he ever did.

Which, it wouldn't be the first time since this Jeanie nonsense began that he hadn't.

Oh, Carol-Ann, I thought, you're nice, you're pretty, you deserve someone who's simply crazy about you.

Like Lloyd.

Like Lloyd had been about me.

For example:

One "Christmas Eve," when I had "stomach thingy," he "called in sick," yelling at "Sergeant Blue" that, yes, "for crapsake," he knew they were "short-staffed due to the holidays," but what "the hey" did that have to do with the fact that "his wife, man" (who Blue *knew* and, Lloyd had always thought, *liked*, having met her that time at "bowling alley") could "barely stand the hell up?" No, sorry, Blue could "shove it," if that's what it came down to, no disrespect intended, sir, but gosh! Then Lloyd slammed the phone down, came over, lifted me up off the couch like I was a baby, sat back down on it with me in his arms, and tenderly put his lips to my head to see if I was still burning up.

Lost in this memory, I stopped short, causing Carol-Ann to *clip-clip-clip* despairingly away down the driveway, taking the orb of her thoughts with her.

I was alone now, just myself, out in the world, free as the breeze.

And soon became aware of a powerful energy.

Like a beckoning call.

Emanating from inside the wedding-house.

From a sort of pantry in there.

In I *whisked*.

The bride and groom had snuck away, and he had her pushed into a corner and they were laughing at how long it was taking for her to hike up her voluminous—

This was not the first time they had *ever*.

But it was the first time they would *today*.

Doing it in the pantry like this, during the reception, was, they felt, proof of the daring, special, epic love-bond between them.

As long as they (yikes) didn't get caught.

In it went. She gasped. From the kitchen came a sound, and they laughed (oh God, this was *too* good, *too* memorable), and out it came, and the groom hustled off into the kitchen to fend off two snooping-around old ladies, by offering to show them the honeymoon brochure, if only he could find the darned thing, señoras, oh, wait, he knew where it was, it was in his jacket, out there in the reception, hanging over his chair at the main table, ladies, so please, come on, follow me!

Oh, the secret thrill of sneaking away.

Oh, the joy of someone wanting you so bad.

Lloyd (muddy "head to toe," just having finished "sled run number 6") flings "cardboard sled" away like it's no longer interesting, given that, you know, here *I* am, and his eyes light up with love, love for *me,* and he picks me up and totes me on his hip over behind the Sinclairs' "garden shed," while back on "patio," "the gang" oohs and whoops and makes "smooching noises" and he whispers, "Jillie, kid, I want to give you what you really want," which I find sort of risqué or racy, to which I go, "Oh, really, Mister Man, maybe this isn't exactly the right time and place?" and his voice goes all soft, like: "Not that, kiddo, no. Well, yes to that, sure, any old time, but what I mean is, well: what you said you really wanted and have been bugging me about since basically day one? I just wanted to tell you that, you know, I'm ready. Whenever you are."

Which, what that meant was: a baby.

Oh, dang, I could've ate that guy alive.

Eek, I was rounding a critical bend now and, tell the truth, felt a tad bit more Jill than not.

And was loving it!

Against my better judgment, just one more:

On "twin bed," in little bedroom, in "duplex," on "Crowne Street," we tried and tried as, in through "open window" came (depending on "direction of wind") "rose-scented breeze" or "garbage-stink" from "alley," or, if "no wind at all," it could be "hot as all get-out," but "little did we care"! All that glorious summer we tried, doing it "every which way," but it hardly seemed like "trying" for the sheer heat-sweaty lovely, longing, grunting, pushing, wanting of it all, and sometimes, from other half of "duplex," "good old Jeri" would pound on the wall, shouting, "At least do it quiet!" But we would not do it quiet. No way. "Sorry, Jer!" Lloyd might shout back. "Come over and join us, kid!"

And from over there Jer would cackle.

Lloyd and I were "love match." So "hot to trot."

Trying and trying all that summer.

That "summer of '76."

That "bicentennial summer."

"Happy Bday America," Jeri's "cute grandbrat," Melinda, had scrawled in red, white, and blue "sidewalk chalk" across "driveway," and, all summer long, Lloyd did his best not to wash "that saying" off, with the hose, out there in "elephant bells" (loose at the bottom, tight at the top) or, sometimes, prework, getting in some early watering, in full cop regalia, before heading down to the station for his dang shift.

The bride, re-situated, rushed out of the pantry.

Into the arms of the groom, who had somehow lost the two old ladies.

Such a kiss.

Such a kiss they shared.

That seemed to promise many happy future days.

And put me in mind of other kisses, from my bygone days.

Of wishing to kiss; of having kissed; of having kissed too much; of having kissed not enough, of lying in "antique four-poster," purchased by "Mother," "on credit," at "Sears," her "favorite store," while imagining being kissed by "Phil Everly," "pop star"; of longing to be kissed (by someone, anyone, please, God) at "junior high skating party"; of sitting in "front seat" of Chevelle, swollen-lipped, joyful, having just been kissed, kissed, kissed by Daniel Masterson, "lab-partner in biology," who, leaving Chevelle as if in a daze, stumbled toward "front door" being held open by his "quizzical-looking mom" ("Valerie"); of (ah, yes, here it was) being kissed *by Lloyd*, for "very first time," at "stock car race" at "Raceway Park," and all at once the "bleacher-seats" beneath us seemed to fall away and my hand was on his "blue-jeaned" leg, there beside "mustard stain," my young mind running wild with thoughts of all the things we might (could, would) do, back in his "Impala," away from all these—

Golly.

Goodness, gosh.

I used to be a person, a full person, with many small memories, small, lovely—

Such as:

In "front entry," on "little credenza," "photos" of "Mom," "Mom and Dad," "me and Dad," and just "Dad" leaning against Chevelle with "cocky look" on face, because "had dimples," because "cute" and knew it.

And:

You held "Barbie" by her legs and "whack-whack-whacked" her against the much-larger "Mrs. Briggs" doll, "Barbie's" way of "pitching a fit" because "Mrs. Briggs" had said no, she was not allowed to climb out of "bathtub" to "go on date."

And:

"Me, Mom, Dad" at "St. Monica's," my little body warming up but just on one side in the many-colored light beaming down from "stained-glass window" showing six gaunt gray "Apostles" pulling a net of fish up into their already fish-tilted boat.

Could make left wrist (but not right) crack by giving it "good hard pop."

In terms of times tables: nines and elevens, easy; twelves not "my cup of tea."

In "big hallway mirror," I looked "so long and pretty," like (Big Deb, mom of my best friend, Little Deb, would say) "a dang gazelle."

In terms of favorites: Color: green; Season: winter; Candy: "Smarties."

Dad, watching me looking up all reverent at those Apostles in that tilted boat, gives me a double-pat on the shoulder, as in: You're good, kid, sure am fond of you, Jillie.

Oh, I felt just sick. I did not want to be THIS THING anymore, this stiff *elevated* THING, but wanted, instead, to be me, sweet ME again, all the way, and for this whole awful dream (of having been blown up/killed/sent all over the place three hundred and forty-three times in all, so far, to a bunch of dying dopes who didn't appreciate me *at all*) to be DONE, so I could be ME again back in that beautiful living body I knew and loved so well and had always so much enjoyed having.

ME, ME again.

With father, mother, friends.

Husband.

Suddenly I knew what I needed to do.

As mentioned, I am vast, unlimited in the range and delicacy of my voice, unrestrained in love, rapid in apprehension, skillful in motion, capable, equally, of traversing, within a few seconds' time, a mile or ten thousand miles.

So it was no effort at all for me to attain great height and speed east by northeast through the remainder of Texas, then through Oklahoma, Missouri, and Illinois, arriving, in the span of a single breath, at the border of lovely Indiana, commencing, then, to sail out along and above the familiar Wabash, veering eastward where it narrowed and met the Patoka, then following the Patoka (thin, brown, laced with fishing sheds, choppy and white with night-swells) to the village of Stanley.

Gosh, I barely recognized the place.

I hung there above it, taking stock of the many ways in which it had changed.

Hat factory: gone.

River: dammed at its westernmost end.

New mall (Chesterfield Commons): vanished entirely.

The hill down which Lloyd and pals had mud-sledded was still a hill but the Sinclairs' rental was gone and that whole area over there was now this ugly new subdivision where three floor plans just repeated and repeated and repeated (Cape Cod/ranch/larger Cape Cod), the whole god-awful mess running out west as far as Union and as far east as Brewer's Launch Lane.

At that wide bend in Sherwood Ave., among that row of scrawny pines was: no Jardine's.

Sherwood Ave. itself: thrice-widened.

That row of scrawny pines: sacrificed in the widening.

It might have been a different town altogether. If not for the baseball field at St. Thomas Aquinas and the alley behind it, which ran (as always) due west, past Turner Park, I never would have been able to find Crowne Street, where our dear little duplex was.

Inside of which Lloyd and I had been a total love match.

So hot to trot.

All that summer.

Summer of '76.

That bicentennial summer.

The summer before my untimely—

Wait.

What?

Where was "duplex"? The entire length of "Crowne Street," including "laundromat," was now an ugly, block-long "Regional Data Center."

Whatever that was!

Lloyd, Lloyd, I thought, where are you, dear? Young, beautiful, tan, broad-shouldered, lifting up the couch with one hand when drunk, just to show me that you could? Dancing around the kitchen, in "cop pants," no shirt, to "Heartsfield" or "Allman Brothers," sitting patiently beside me as we colored in, with those big honker marker-pens, "Fantasy Forest," the paint-by-number your mother gave us the day we got engaged.

Speaking of Shirley, Lloyd's mother, I *whisked* at once to "Shirley's house," i.e., the home of my "mom-in-law," i.e., Lloyd's mother, Shirley.

But *whisking* thoroughly around inside, found: no Shirley, and all the furniture new and different, kind of huge, rather "mod," and a young couple was in there and some new kind of music was blaring, all wonks and whistles like "robot" might make, in a kitchen that was missing one wall and had gained another, and they were happy, with no memory of any Shirley whatsoever, as they had bought the house not from her, but from the Verhagens, Tom and Kate.

Up in the attic, behind a concealing rafter, I found the one and only item in the place that had the slightest thing to do with me: a box, and inside it, my wedding dress, wrapped in tissue paper, and written on the box, in my handwriting (!), were the words: "J&L wedding, 1975," plus a cartoon I'd drawn of two smiling hearts holding hands.

That had been such a great day.

Everyone so happy for us and all.

There in "clearing" in "Yankee Woods."

Beneath "wedding tent" from "Rent-A-Tent."

I shot out through the wall, landed on "Shirley's lawn," where "cute fake well" (with "little clay donkey") used to be but was no more.

Why had my darling wedding dress been just left up in that dumb musty attic like that?

Where was Lloyd?

Where was he?

*

I emitted the shrill repetitive shrieking one of our ilk will emit if wishing to attract others of our ilk for consultation.

A crowd soon gathered.

Some of whom I knew (Jen Ballard, who I used to babysit, all grown up now, albeit dead; Mr. Mendon, the creep from the drugstore, who could sometimes be nice; Lisa Childs, the cheerleader who'd fallen off the Ferris wheel at Melody Lake while tipsy; eight petite gymnasts from Stanley High, whose bus had overturned coming home from "away game," who had, it seemed, ever since, been holding hands), some I didn't know (a threadbare fellow with a musket and a pamphlet; four wiry drowned Iroquois toting a canoe with a busted-out bottom; many simple Indiana working folks, hats in their hands, trying, eternally, to loosen the fancy, too-tight dress clothes in which they'd been buried; a short, fat priest with a goatee who rushed from person to person, urging repentance, but he had this very annoying voice and now, as in life, that voice was causing people to turn away from him while trying not to laugh, and hence no one at all was getting saved).

Forward stepped my grandmother, in the faded green housedress she'd worn pretty much constantly there at the end.

Grandma Gust, we'd called her. Because of her late-life farting. She'd been the first to call herself that. After ripping one at dinner. And then we all picked up on it.

It was actually so funny.

Sweetest grandma ever.

Yes, dear? she said.

Lloyd? I said. Lloyd Blaine.

Grandma cocked her head.

As if in thought.

Then rose, and the others fell in behind her, and I behind them.

We flew west across Stanley, to a part of town that used to be its own separate village, Hickum, but then got absorbed into the greater town of Stanley, and was known, in my day, for two bars (Jocko's and the Maze), both of which would let a high school kid (even one as baby-faced as me, with no ID, not even a fake) just waltz right in.

Behind Jocko's lay (my heart dropped) the broad expanse of the cemetery.

Sacred Heart of Mary Cemetery. Down we all floated as one.

Beneath a willow, fifteen feet from a stone bench upon which that Slurpee cup rested and had been resting now for the better part of a year, was the same old (disappointingly economical) stone reading: J BLAINE, WIFE, 1954–1976.

There beside it was (oh dear) a new one, made of marble, not just plain old stone, reading: L BLAINE, HUSBAND, 1948–2023.

I dived down underground before I'd really thought it through, and there he—

And shot back out so quick I found myself up on a phone line, sobbing, and though I had zero bodyweight, the phone line was swaying ever so slightly just from the sheer power of my feelings.

Those others of our ilk rose up, forming around me a consoling cloud.

He went, I said.

Yes, Grandma said. Right away. Immediately after. No dilly-dallying.

Without finding me first, I said.

Right, she said.

Without saying goodbye, I said.

And there's more, Grandma said.

There was.

Over on the far side of Lloyd's stone was another (of the same ritzy marble), reading: SUSAN CONNOR BLAINE, WIFE & MOTHER, 1951–2022, and at the base of it lay this bouquet of fresh roses, and propped against the bouquet was an old photo, of her, SUSAN, when still young, with three little kids, each kid looking, around the eyes, like Lloyd, and Lloyd was in the photo too, super-happy, also young, that is, not all that much older than he'd been when he and I had—

Had parted ways.

Due to me getting blown up and all.

There was one more thing I needed to know.

Go ahead, said Grandma.

Paul Bowman, I said.

What about him? she said.

Jail? I said.

Grandma cocked her head.

No, she said.

Caught? I said.

Never, she said. Still lives in that same old house.

Still alive, I said.

Almost ninety, she said. Not even sorry. Barely remembers doing it. Over the years, he made it okay with himself. In his mind. You know.

Oh, I said.

More or less forgave himself, she said.

Thanks, I said.

Made himself the victim of the story, she said. Rationalized it. The way people tend to—

All right, all right, I said.

Also, look there, said Grandma.

Here were the graves of my mother and father, both of whom had still been alive and sort of young when I'd gotten blown up.

Couldn't have been easy for them.

Seeing their graves was the hardest blow of all.

I used to come in from school and there they'd be. They used to come in from being out, at dinner maybe, and there I'd be, on the couch, older now, old enough to be left home alone, and I'd jump up and run over, so happy to see them. And we'd do a family hug there by the Jesus in our niche.

Once there'd been no me and then they'd come along and made me and now I was gone and they were too.

It hurt.

Really hurt.

Maybe it's time, Grandma said, indicating my grave with her cane.

I dived down, had a look at that desiccated brownish-green figure of medium height (length), cleaved in half at approximately the hip-line, left arm disconnected at the shoulder, a fuzz-beard of mold on what was left of its cheekbones, wearing, still, the outfit Lloyd had picked out (beige skirt, pale pink blouse, black pumps, my favorite in life, a fact Lloyd had sweetly remembered even in his grief).

I shot back up.

(No bun in oven.

By the way.)

No, I said.

Why not? Grandma said. What keeps you here, Doll?

What keeps *you* here? I said.

She leaned forward to answer, as if about to tell me some long-kept secret.

Then did a little fart, like in the old days, so we might part on good terms.

And off she went.

Off they all went, to their various afterlife tasks.

I stood there looking around.

What was I doing?

What was I doing *here,* in this crappo graveyard, in this ugly little town that could never mean anything to me again?

I'd received the gift of *elevation* from our great God in Heaven himself.

And this was how I behaved?

Elevation was true. It was. For sure.

Me, *elevated*? Was real. Realer by a mile, at this point, than "Jill 'Doll' Blaine."

All righty then, I thought.

Gosh, golly, embarrassing.

I must put her behind me forever, that girl who once was, then was no more, and would never be again.

Up I shot and raced back across Illinois and Missouri and then entered Oklahoma.

As I may have mentioned, it was sometimes good, when rattled, to think in the highest possible register. And, by this, regain *elevation.*

So:

The porch light of a farmhouse outside Tulsa threw a chute of yellow light out across its rough lawn, as if intending the light-chute to be taken for a path to the farm's white-fenced goat-pen.

But something was off.

I dropped, flew the length of the goat-pen, exciting the goats therein by my presence; heads humbly lowered, they fled to positions against the glowing white fence, propelled there by my strangeness.

Nope, still rattled.

And, as far as *elevation:* no, not great, pretty subpar.

I felt weird, dual, not quite right.

In my mind was a dispute, like two women were up there competing for, so to say, a certain right, the right to guide the ship of speech.

It was like *she* (the *elevated*, more or less hoity-toity part, no offense) kept pushing *me* (who had actually once *lived* and all) out of the way, even as we, together, had to admit that she (the *elevated* part) could, really could, say, more precisely than I could, that which we felt might need expressing.

It seemed I'd somehow damaged myself on that stupid trip to Indiana.

Had become, it felt like, a bit of a freak.

A freak of sorts.

A hybrid.

Part *elevated*, part Jill "Doll" Blaine.

This had never happened before, not so extremely, and I have to say I didn't much like it.

And tried again to fix it.

Dropping, I skimmed along the surface of a red-clay stream feeding the Canadian River that, flowing along there in the dark, was rippled by a wheat-stalk-flattening cross-breeze that set four wind-chimes to sounding from the front porch of a creepy hunter's shack/shed I wouldn't have set foot inside of if you gave me a million bucks, honestly.

Dang, it was so odd.

To find oneself in this new mixed mode.

What a riot.

Confounding yet intriguing.

Weird as all get-out.

I couldn't seem to shake Jill "Doll" Blaine (all she'd seen, been, and done) and didn't want to. But neither could Jill "Doll" Blaine shake me, the *elevated* part, and didn't want to, for to be in touch even briefly with *elevation* is to know the bliss of being one with God.

In any event, I had to get back to it.

Here, now, was Texas, here the neighborhood of my charge.

Every room on the second floor of his house was lit, though only one of them was in use.

I landed softly, in a sitting position, on the base of the statue of the golden dog.

I couldn't go in.

Just couldn't somehow.

Needed a minute.

Up the driveway came a man of our ilk, short but densely muscled, shirtless, who looked as if he'd been rolling around in a vat of grease, whose wild white hair was sticking straight up.

Seen my wife? he said. I'm always about ten minutes behind her. Old lady in a rocking chair. Or young gal with her hair down all slutty, about to dash off into the rain. To meet her friends. Also sluts.

Afraid not, I said.

I mean to make it up to her good and proper, he said.

Do you, I said.

Naw, he said. I mean to do what I want with her again, way I used to. I'll catch her. If you see her? Knock her down, pin her down, and hold her for me, will you?

No, I said.

Maybe I'll pin you down, he said.

I blasted through him, thinking, as I did, of a huge mound of shit coming out of his rear, with razor blades embedded in it.

When I came out on the other side, he was on the ground, moaning in pain, clutching his ass.

All right, all right, he said. I was just funnin' you.

Go "fun" someone else, I said. I'm not in the mood.

I guess not, he said.

And he tried to stand but his ass hurt too much.

How'd you do that? he said.

Not sure, I said.

But that wasn't true.

I had a pretty good idea.

Part of me was eternal and I had *those* considerable powers at hand (my mind was vast, unlimited, unrestrained, rapid, and skillful), while the other part, which very much longed to be alive again, was making me: desirous, ornery, active, aching to interfere in whatever way I could, in any old thing.

Powerful combo.

Nearby, someone was whistling "La Marseillaise."

The Frenchman came unsteadily around the side of the house.

Ah, *madame,* he said. Here you are. Where have you been?

You look wonderful, by the way. Disordered, loose. Full of desire and confusion. Rather unhinged. Yet beautiful. In a rough way.

Oh, be quiet, I said.

But it was true: my beige skirt and pale pink blouse had been cleaned and pressed by fresh love for life and also I had self-redone my hair with fondness for ME, and, being decidedly ephemeral yet nevertheless touched by the eternal, I looked, if I may say so, just *terrific*.

He, on the other hand, looked awful: his head a nearly featureless blob, his hands two vague smears at the ends of sticklike arms, his feet likewise, at the ends of sticklike legs, his formerly white clothing/boots/scarf now dirt-colored and in tatters.

You don't look so good, I said.

I don't feel so good, he said.

Suddenly he noticed the fellow whose ass I'd damaged.

What happened to him? he said.

Me, I said. I did.

You are perhaps not yourself? he said.

Which was like the understatement of the century.

The fellow whose ass I'd damaged got to his feet and limped away, one hand reflexively covering his damaged ass.

Have a great night, I said.

Madame, the Frenchman said urgently. I feel I must return at once, to that place to which those of our ilk must retreat when in need of—

Sure, sure, no problem, I said, and scooped him up.

Merci, he said.

Then kissed me.

Impulsively.

On the cheek.

But still.

Given the unusual state of his body, it was like being kissed by a lipless, eager ball. But it was pleasant enough. To be kissed again. After all this time. Or, I should say, pleasant enough to have someone arrange his luminous head-blop in such a way that, had we been mortal, he would have been kissing me.

I find you attractive, he said. Suddenly.

Not surprising, I said.

What's happening? he said. I hope you're not getting yourself into trouble.

Don't sweat it, I said.

Into the driveway pulled "taxicab."

"Taxi."

Taxi, yes.

Centralizing my considerable strength, holding in my heart the intention of sending the Frenchman back to that place to which those of our ilk must retreat when in need of a fresh beginning, I exploded him upward.

Off he went: smaller, smaller, gone.

A middle-aged woman got out of the taxi, paid the driver, crossed to the statue of the golden dog, uttered a few words to it, trying, it seemed, to delay her entry until she might compose herself.

I leapt up, passed through the wall of the bedroom, crouched quietly beside my charge's bed, waited there.

Julia's here, his wife called from the landing.

I heard the front door open, then a hushed greeting, the wife's crisp summary of the situation, the sound of the new arrival advancing up the stairs.

Then: a flash of blond hair, plain features elaborately made up; dazzling green eyes, solid build, a golden cross around her neck.

She rushed across the room, dropped to her knees, kissed my charge on the cheek.

Oh, gosh, Daddy, she whispered. You don't look so hot, pard. How are you? How's everything going? My flight was good. Pretty good. We had some turbulence, which, honestly, about scared the dang pants—

Leaning in closer, taking in his stillness, his pallor, his shallow, rapid breathing, she began thinking in a hushed, urgent, prayerlike whisper, feeling that, in his diminished state (more spirit than flesh, so close to the end) he might be able to receive it.

And he was. He was able to receive it.

As (edging into the conjoined orb of their thoughts) was I.

Were we.

The two of us, Jill and non-Jill, now one, mutually resolved to fall silent and listen.

First, okay, she wanted him to know he'd been the best daddy ever. She'd been crazy about him ever since her earliest days, when he'd come in smelling of cigarettes and the road and cheeseburgers and motor oil and pick her up over his head and fly her around the room while Momma kept saying, The lamp, the lamp, K.J., mind her little-bitty head!

Second: she understood that his early life had been hard and that was why he'd sometimes been a little harsh. And demanding. And sometimes—Daddy, she had to say it—rude. Rude to her friends, rude to her prom date, Randy, that one time.

That had been—she had to say it—rough.

But the thing was: she forgave it. Forgave it all. She wanted him to know that. He'd made her strong. Yes he had. By being so difficult. And often unfair. Because look at her now: she took no bull-hockey from anybody, and if a person was being rude to her or trying to bully her?

She kicked butt, took names later.

So, thank you.

Thank you, Daddy, for that.

Daddy, if you can hear me?

Thank you.

What she wanted to say, what she'd *come* here to say? What she truly believed? Was: Good job, you! Well done! Thou hast been a great warrior and accomplisher and hath— Daddy, you did great things, I mean it. You started low, out there in cowboy country, for Lord's sake, then went forth and won big while opening up many, many cans of whoop-butt on all who would oppose you.

And gave us a *great* life. You did. Truly. We traveled all over the world, always first-class, did things none of my friends at school ever got to—well, most of them, anyway, given that some of my friends at school were also, like us, doing pretty darn well—but, Daddy: London, Moscow, Kenya, Bethlehem, all before I was twenty?

Although, yes, true, she'd taken some guff in high school from some of the liberal kids, because of his job, which— Lordy, don't get her wrong, she was not now, and never had been, a lib. She didn't want him thinking that. She believed in this country, and in positive values and taking responsibility for oneself, like he'd taught her, and saw zero use in complaining or looking only at the negative side of things or pissing and moaning about every little hardship the way the libdopes tended to do, as if nothing in life was fun or beautiful or a cause for joy and everything was a terrible dang guilty burden to bear. (And, yes, Daddy: she and her church friends used "libdope" now, not "libtard," not because of p.c. but because "libdope" seemed somehow kinder, more in keeping with the teachings.)

Anyway: her worldview was solid. She wanted him to know that. She'd recovered from her brief, friend-induced flirtation with libtarditude. Dopitude, rather. Especially after that batshit gal at the country club had implied she was a racist. Too much!

Just because a person mistook one black waitress for another, did that make her a racist?

It was too much, libdopes.

Back it on down.

She loved everybody just the same, like he'd taught her: white people, brown people, red people, gay folks, those two indistinguishable black (or Black, she guessed you had to say now) waitresses, even the young white-trash/trailer-girl waitress who'd called her racist, although, as far as that lowlife, she had to admit she was going to have to really work at loving that dipshit, or even letting her wait on her ever again, because, when you really thought about it, wasn't that white girl being racist herself, against whites, by coming after her the way she had, literally pulling her into the coat-check closet, just seething with self-righteousness, wearing way too much makeup, with a nose ring like an enraged baby bull and one of her blocky ugly waitress shoes untied? Coming after her so hard that the Black waitress she'd mistaken for that other Black waitress had to come racing in and pull that White biotch off her?

Anyway.

(Oh, he loved listening to her. Always had. The two of them

would stay at the table after dinner and she'd talk and talk, about things at school, world events, which trees she liked more than others, and so on. Smart kid. Knew her own mind.)

Look, she was just going to say it: he was dying. Okay? Sometimes, dying people got trapped in denial. And denial? Takes a lot of energy. This friend of hers at church? Did hospice. She said that if a loved one present could sort of sound the gong, you know, saying, in effect: It's happening, really happening, to *you*, *now*? That was good. A good thing.

According to Cara.

Her friend from church who did hospice.

Was she making things worse? By being so frank? She could stop. If it bothered him. But one thing she'd learned (through counseling, yes, but also at Bible study) was:

God does not like *closed*.

God does not do *denial*.

You know who opened up big-time there at the end? Our Lord. Jesus Christ. Dying, He'd called out to His Father to forgive His enemies, who were, literally, at that moment, up there on Golgotha, killing Him. He knew He was dying and had the presence of mind to wonder: How might I, even in this dreadful moment, continue to serve? While there, below, at the foot of His cross, stood His enemies, the terrible Romans, leering up at Him with their big old pikes and swords and horrid strappy sandals and pointy helmets and whatnot. Could he, her daddy, do that, here and now? Forgive his many enemies? The many enemies who had, over the years, opposed him, including those mysterious dumbasses who'd left a buttload of *dead seagulls* on their lawn once, during the whole *Galatea* spill crisis thingamabob when she was in junior high, which, by the way, had been just super for her social life, and thanks y'all protesters for that, and could he forgive, also, those morons in the media, and those trolls who'd sent, over the years, just an endless stream of *terrible* letters, calling him, among other things, "corporate pig," "godless seeker of Mammon," and "tone-deaf monster," when really what he was, was not a monster at all, but just a tiny sweet little old thing (always the smallest of all the other daddies), who'd (crabbily, but still) taught her how to change a flat out there in their garage and had shown up, unannounced, when she was eight, at her Junior Miss Bowling class, and bought every single girl there a Coke, and insisted that every last girl finish hers, so as not to be wasteful, even, unfortunately, that one girl, Lydia, who, it turned out, was diabetic?

Maybe they should pray.

Could she pray with him a bit?

You good with that, Daddy? she whispered aloud. Should we maybe pray a little?

(He tried to say he'd be happy to pray. But nothing came out.)

Hearing nothing, she charged ahead.

Thank you, Lord, for the gift of this man, she prayed. Through his mighty efforts, the world has been much changed. He traveled far and wide, over every continent. Praise that. Worked with so many different kinds of folks. Amen. Was just terrific at, uh, taking a unit or division and, um, as she understood it, making it more efficient, or profitable? By trimming things back, kind of ruthlessly, and, uh, getting rid of the, like, dead wood? Which, come to think of it, was another group of enemies he might consider forgiving: those two hundred numbnuts he'd fired just before Christmas that one super-cold winter, who'd formed a sad little club and sometimes came over together, all wearing parkas, to picket their dang house.

She remembered that nice one, Wanda, who used to sneak little waves over at her and had once pulled her aside to slip her a Perfume Patty.

Lord, forgive him. For any and all mistakes he'd made. Like when he was gone overseas for three straight months her senior year. Or the way he'd kept snapping at Randy, her earlier-mentioned prom date, just because Randy had done his science fair project on electric cars and was sort of fired up about it. Randy had been *seventeen*, Daddy. Was it so important that he be proven wrong? On the night of her prom? Necessary for you to drag Randy over to the whiteboard in the kitchen and throw all those numbers at him and mock him out as he stood there sweating, nervously pressing her corsage so tightly against his rented ruffled shirt that he ended up crushing it, and then he'd slid that ugly flat thing on her wrist and they'd had a miserable time all night because he kept defending his original calculations?

Forgive him for all of that, Lord.

Also?

For all those questionable things he'd supposedly possibly done.

Per that stupid documentary.

That Fran had made her watch.

Daddy, remember Fran? From grad school? Super-nervous gal? Owned a big old lake house? Or, used to? Up in Minnesota? But then: two straight months of rain, in July, and here came the lake, rising, rising, and pretty soon: no lake house. Or, less of one. After that, Fran had gone a little eco-wacky. And had done this sort of intervention. On her (!). In Vegas. On a trip that was supposed to be fun (!). Fran had tricked her. Into watching that video. Fran'd sat there watching her watch it.

After, Fran had said that maybe she, Julia, might want to issue some kind of public statement. Or post an apology on Instagram or whatever? Or donate to an environmental charity? In her dad's name?

As if.

As if, bitcharoo.

She'd broken with Fran. Fran was dead to her.

There was no way.

No. Flipping. Way.

That he'd done those things.

Or, if he had done them that he'd known they were bad.

Or, if he had known they were bad—

God, why did everyone have to be so *mean* about everything, anyhow?

Hello, he was in the *oil business*, Fran, dunce. The *business* of *oil*. Okay? Finding it, getting it out of the ground or wherever, selling it. How did you, Fran, physically get to the Minnesota lake house, when you still had it, dimwit? How did you make your way out of Minnesota and across Wisconsin, Illinois, Indiana, Ohio, Pennsylvania, New York, Massachusetts that one autumn to see the Magritte show in Boston you ended up being so crazy about? How did you get to that bat mitzvah in Palm Springs that was so "transcendent" it made you "rethink your ideas regarding the value of ceremony" or that wedding in Maui that had the fire jugglers, one of whom, supposedly, you made out with?

You drove, you flew, you kombucha-making hypocrite.

And yet.

And yet.

Daddy, she whispered. Do you have any idea? What people are saying? About you? On TV and the internet and in so many articles and books and podcasts lately? Is it true? All of it? Any of it? If so, maybe you were a darker, trickier bastard than I ever—

Not "bastard."

Guy.

Not "darker."

Complicated.

Not "trickier."

Secretive.

A much more complicated, secretive guy than I ever—

If so, if you did know, and did it anyway? Which, if I'm being frank, I feel was probably, yes, the case? It breaks my heart, and I have to say, because I want, if we are really parting, for us to do so from a place of total honesty:

It disappoints me, Daddy.

Disappoints me greatly.

I just feel really let down by you.

I always saw you as someone who tried to do what was right, no matter what, so this is a truly hard pill for me to—

Pausing for a look down at my charge, she noted that his hair, badly in need of cutting, was, just a little bit, in the front there, shaking, or quaking, or whatever.

Just slightly moving with the motion of his frail old body.

Now the shaking stopped and he went completely still and it occurred to her that (good Christ) she'd killed him.

With this selfish last-minute bitchfest.

Then his lips slightly moved, as if he were trying to moisten them.

Oh, thank God.

Lord, forget it, they could talk about it later.

Or not.

She took the washcloth from the bedside table, dipped it into his water glass, wet his lips.

There you go.

There you go, sweetie.

She leaned over, kissed his head.

My charge, for the first time since I'd known him, managed to speak aloud.

Devil, he mumbled.

Say what now? she said. The devil's not in here, Daddy. That's just your meds.

Lady, he said.

Are you saying there's a lady devil in here? she said.

From deep in his throat he managed a sound of affirmation.

Okay, she said. All right. What we need here is some rest, I think. Or wait, you know what? Let's do this.

She brought her hands together.

Heavenly Father, she said. Help my daddy out here. Devil lady? Be gone. Any and all devils, be gone. Give my daddy some peace, y'all.

All the devils many wrong in here tonight, he said.

Alarmed, she rushed to the landing and called down to her mother to get up here, now, *please,* because, one, he was awake and talking, and two, from the sound of it, things were getting sort of— Could she, Momma, please get up here *now,* please, stat, pronto, thank you?

Hearing no response from her mother, she left the room and pounded down the stairs to find her.

Not a devil, I said.

He let out a low groan.

Actual groan.

Had his daughter or wife been in the room, they would have heard it.

More than anything that had preceded it (the bird onslaught, his interactions with the Pennsylvania girl, Miss Eva, his father, Ed Dell) this had stung him. By this, his enemies had won. They'd succeeded in turning his only child against him. They'd poured poison into her ear and she'd believed them. She was his dear girl, constant defender, biggest fan. And now, for the rest of her life, long as she lived, she was going to think of him like that?

In that way?

As that guy?

A darker, trickier bastard than she'd ever—

No.

Jesus, no.

What he needed to do was hop out of this bed and go downstairs and fetch the bag of black licorice stashed above the fridge and sit that gal down and say: Cupcake, whatever beef you've got with me, it's because you had it all handed to you on a silver platter, which is why half the time you don't have any damn idea of how things work out in the real world, angel, I'm sorry to say, and why you have, all your life, been easily misled by people who meant you no good and were trying to take advantage of your kind nature, sweet pea. So, sit down, let's talk this thing out.

He became aware of me again.

You reading my mind? he said.

Yes, I said.

I want you to stop it, he said.

No, I said.

You seem different, he said.

I am different, I said. I'm Jill. Jill Blaine. Jill "Doll" Blaine.

Weren't you always? he said.

Not this much, I said.

From downstairs came the sound of his daughter crying hysterically, her mother comforting her, a glass breaking, a sudden silence.

What's all that about? he said.

I smiled a sad smile.

No, he thought. This wasn't it. Couldn't be. Not yet. His death was meant to take place in an ancient stone mansion. A gray manse on a misty moor. In Europe somewhere. Like in a 1940s movie. He'd always thought that. Why had he always thought that? No idea. He just had. All across the property his peasants would be weeping. In the doorway a butler was trying not to cry. Like that. The doctor with whom he'd aways played chess was racing to him by horse-drawn sleigh through a blizzard. The village luminaries had gathered around his bedside. He'd always been the best among them. Finally, they saw it. It didn't hurt. It was Death but it didn't hurt. He was just growing increasingly tired and philosophical.

Next stop, Heaven, where everyone would be waiting: Grandpa, Mee-Mee, Mother and Father, Uncle Theo; Norman, his older cousin and first confidant, killed in Korea; Bip Wren, crushed on a rig in Debolt County. Well done, would be the consensus up there, great job, K.J., you were right all along, and even if some found you too overbearing/powerful/decisive, we, up here in Heaven, always approved of everything you did and were with you all the way. You were always the grown-up in every room. Sometimes babies need to be picked up and moved away from dangers they're too idiotic to grasp. Ditto with subordinates, underlings, the public.

There was a world to run, and you ran it, K.J.

Bravo, congrats, many thanks.

Now, grab you some Heavenly grub. Name your poison. A heightened version of the best meal you ever had? Sure, here you go: Paris, 1986, scallops but looking pretty as a dessert, gold leaf sprinkled over the top. An exact re-creation of that special birthday meal Mother whipped up when you turned ten? Steak, fried potatoes, angel food cake with whipped cream and strawberries and afterward Mother let you have a sip of her wine out on the porch swing? Eat up, please enjoy. That had been back in the days when he'd sometimes go wading after school in Crow Creek. Having missed the bus, he'd walk home in wet trousers, only to catch all kind of heck from Mother upon arrival, including the belt. Which, in those days, was common. And nobody minded about the so-called violence of that.

Much.

Once a salamander from the creek hopped out of his pantcuff and sent Mother dashing into the bedroom wailing at the top of her lungs.

Wait.

This was no gray manse on a misty moor.

Where was he?

Where the hell was he?

The Colorado place? Which they'd always called, for some reason, "the château"? Some château. Last time they were up there, there'd been a big pile of tires behind it. Little Joel'd better get that goddamned tire pile gone or he'd be looking for a new position.

Well, this wasn't the château.

And it wasn't Key West and wasn't Maui. The elegant Minton place? No, the Minton place had burned down on Halloween, tail end of Vietnam. Couzens Hall, second floor, his freshman-year dorm room, freshly painted? With the clanking radiator? Lying here in his quiet dorm, he couldn't wait. He could do it, he could do all of it. The untainted semester lay ahead. He'd made a vow to attend every home game this fall. Had saved up, bought a special new sweater in maize and blue, school colors.

But no.

Hang on there.

Christ, where was he? How old was Julia? There'd be a clue in that. Three, four? Bangs cut straight across, cute as a bug? Recently they'd all pulled up together in front of the Sammons Center: him, Viv, Julia. Yes, right: he'd snapped at the Mexican kid there, No wheelchair, get away, *ya no lo necesitamos.* Julia had been driving. Driving the Mercedes.

So, she couldn't be three, a kid wasn't allowed to drive at—

Ah, God, it all came back: he was old, sick, had endured months of just the most horrendous degrading crap: scans, chemo, different chemo, more scans, blood work, ports, stitches from when he'd fallen in the bathroom, endless consultations after the stitches got infected, the first operation, then the second, and then he'd gone blind in the eye in front of the tumor, had fallen again (stitches in a different part of his face), and started throwing absolutely everything up and then came the news that—well, no more chemo. Had the tumor shrunk? No, not at all, and also? He might lose that eye. Thanks, thanks so much, you merciless quacks. The cancer was everywhere. In one shoulder, down the spine, in the liver, the bladder, you name it. How about my shoes? he'd said. No, the nurse said wryly, your shoes are fine. He'd been short with her once too often. Chubby bimbo. Squat incompetent. He didn't care if she was Ethiopian or Ugandan or whatnot. More power to her on that front. No: he cared that she was such a goddamned bitch to him all the time. In his prime he'd have gobbled her up and spit her out. Now he needed her. He reached over, touched her hand. As if they were equals. She wasn't having it. Curled her lip like she smelled something off. Had they given up on him, then? No, no, they had not, she said, they were referring him to Sovereign and the great folks over there.

To which he'd said, Hospice? Good God, are you serious?

She was. Serious.

Serious as a heart attack.

And now he was diapered, he recalled grimly. Him. He was. K. J. Boone was. A team of changers swooped down on him four times a day in the sudden smell of asswipes and the sound of efficient under-the-breath coordination. "Got a little something on the, uh, inner leg, Janie." The Russian guy lifting him up at the hip with one gloved hand while the Boston-sounding gal reached under him and—

The air-con came on now with a familiar *whump* and air began flowing out of it. He could picture the exact grating on the vents. Ack, this was the house on Owl Flight Terrace. In Dallas. Jesus Christ, he knew every inch of it. He was in the guest bedroom, second floor. Why was he in here? In the Slop Room? Why wasn't he in his own goddamned room? Had he worked so hard all these years just to end up croaking in the Slop Room? He'd speak to someone about this. Or have Viv do it.

Who was "Viv" again?

Your wife, you dope, he answered himself.

She was here. Viv was. Right here. Julia too.

He was eighty-seven.

Eighty-seven goddamn years old.

All done.

He'd done it all.

It was finished.

His breath was labored and shallow, his internal organs barely functioning, his blood flow had almost ceased, his heart was beating irregularly, like an afterthought.

He was moments from death and knew it.

Into the room came a feeling of dread, as if some livid part of the universe had been summoned and, regardless of who or what must be broken in the process, intended to establish that it, and not the other (merciful, loving) part reigned supreme.

Jill was still very much within me.

Not-Jill was still very much within me.

We were an inseparable unity, no longer *we,* but *I.*

And resolved henceforth to think and act as one.

Present in my charge was a desire to confess something he'd previously been withholding.

Go ahead, I said.

Don't hold me to this, he said. Spitballing.

Go, I said.

And he stopped speaking to me and began reasoning in my direction, as it were.

All right, look, what if he had? (he began).

Made some mistakes?

Let's say (just say, for the sake of argument) that he'd been "wrong." About certain things. Wrong in arguing against a view that now, more and more, seemed to have become, by some sort of public consensus, the prevailing/mainstream view. A view supported by the (yes, he could say it now) apparent increase (anecdotal, but still) in the frequency of certain extreme weather events, occurring so frequently recently that, before his illness, he'd gotten in the habit of turning off the news before the weather came on. The weather made him anxious. He felt blamed by it. Which was absurd, but. Then the weather had started bleeding over into the real news. So he'd stopped watching the news. Who needed it? Nothing new under the sun.

Who needed to see, for example, the filthy, storm-surging Mississippi flooding a kid's birthday party, at which some photographer, intent on tugging heartstrings, had found (*arranged*, more likely) a cluster of pink birthday hats on a little tabletop floating away downriver? Not new. Well, all right, kind of new. But he didn't need to see it. Or some African grandma in her scorched field of cassava or whatnot, toddling up to the camera with a dented cup, begging for something, anything. Or in France, a house absolutely zipping down a hillside through a gauntlet of still-standing houses, the street a sluice of sorts, the scale of the thing just amazing. In Peru, a drone flew over (and over and over) burned-out foundations of home after home, in the driveways of which sat smoldering cars, and between two of the cars stumbled a doe who'd caught fire, fur singed black, and then she dropped in a heap, braying plaintively from her unnervingly wide-open mouth. (Tough, tough to watch, nobody wanted to see that.) In Carmel, the Pacific swept this frail old fart right off his feet (tsunami, Japan) and when his equally frail wife went to help him, the ocean took her and her walker too, and you heard, on the video, someone say: Are they gone? And someone else said: Are they coming back? And a third person, possibly their adult son, started screaming bloody murder and the newscaster said, Could this, too, be considered climate-related?

Having a pretty good idea what the answer was going to be, he'd turned the goddamn set off.

It was all a sort of enviro-porn and he didn't need it. It wasn't scientific, it was conjectural, it implied specious connections between A and B. There were, yes, for sure, strange things happening, but to blame it all so simplistically on one specific cause, one particular—

Shitsake, you did your best. You staked out a certain position. That was how science worked. It was called *having a hypothesis.* Having staked out that position, you defended it. What supported that position was "good," what threatened it was "bad." That was called *human nature.* When you were in charge of a thing, you did your best to protect the interests of that thing. That was called *acting as a responsible corporate steward.*

What had he done that was so goddamn terrible? (By "he" he meant "they," the company of which he'd been in charge, with which he, by dint of years of unstinting, selfless toil, had become synonymous; in a sense, yes, he *was* the company, and so be it, that had always been a source of great pride for him.) Had he funded certain scientists? With whom he agreed? Whose views happened to align with his? To perform certain analyses and write scholarly articles summarizing the results? Guilty as charged. Had he (had they) promoted the resulting articles far and wide? Sure, you bet. He'd believed in the opinions expressed. Or had, at any rate, believed that getting those opinions out in the world did a certain kind of vital work, by way of offering a more well-rounded picture than was, at that time, being presented by the mainstream media, which tended to demonize, oversimplify—

(Speed it up, I said. Your time is short.)

Had he (had they) helped place those articles in prominent newspapers and whatnot? Had he (they) quoted from those favorable articles, in full-page ads that he paid for, in the larger papers of the day, and in glossy brochures widely distributed, somewhat omitting (often for reasons of space) the (some might say) tricky provenance of said articles/studies, as well as any mention of certain simplifications/exaggerations/omissions that had possibly been made? He was proud to say that, in his role as its steward, yes, he'd always done his best to protect his organization from partial truths being lazily disseminated by non-disinterested parties that, left unchallenged, would have endangered the livelihood of thousands of good folks, not to mention the world's critical supply of—

Look, hadn't his enemies (also) cherry-picked, exaggerated, stretched the truth, worked the media, funded organizations friendly to their view?

He'd had the same exact information as everyone else. So why was he the fall guy? The central villain? The "single worst agent in the monumental and criminal effort to deny blah blah blah"?

And what was he supposed to do about it now anyway? At the hour of his death? Cut bait and run? Slink around to the other side of the table, where his enemies gloatingly sat, and cheerily call out: Hey, guess what, get this, you folks were right all along, I was wrong, I'm sorry?

"Oilman K. J. Boone Recants on Deathbed"?

No.

Not happening.

And anyway, if he did recant, who'd know?

You?

You, ghost?

Ghost of some former waitress?

Is that it? I said, a bit coldly. All done? Any more secrets?

No, he said. That's it.

As if in response, the room suddenly throbbed with presence and began rapidly filling with individuals of our ilk: the collective dead from this part of Texas and adjacent areas of Louisiana, Arkansas, and Oklahoma, plus a few who'd died in the Gulf or drifted over from Mexico.

These were real.

That is, not being made by his mind.

I could tell by their transparency, their restlessness, their particularity:

Smocks, car-coats, rain-slickers made of oilcloth; crude boots, glowing loafers, tennis shoes both new and beat-up, sandals, jellies, shoes the poor had fashioned out of cardboard, bare feet callused with walking; skirts, dresses, shirts, and jeans; heads of dirty matted hair, heads of long flowing waist-length black hair, close-cropped scalps, hats covered with dirt, wild feathered headdresses, old Spanish helmets, veils pinned into the hair of demure Catholic ladies; scarred legs, heart-shaped calf muscles, clenching and unclenching fists; a confusion of umbrellas, ranging from crude nineteenth-century models to sleek new ones the likes of which I'd never seen, which folded up neatly to the size of a purse.

When the room was entirely full, the newcomers overflowed into the hallway, then into the stairwell, then down onto the ground floor and, when the whole house was full, into the yard, and even into the yard next door, where, as they stood unseen among the wedding guests, their attention (despite the revelry going on all around them) stayed riveted, always, on my charge's window.

Crowded, he said.

Normal, I said. Happens every time.

Every time what? he said.

Then, on something like a bier, or litter, or royal palanquin, a young man was passed up through the crowd until, somehow perceiving that he'd arrived at his intended destination, he stepped off the litter, moved to the bed, and, standing a bit unsteadily, gazed down at my charge.

Who recognized him immediately.

It was—good God. The curly-haired college kid. From Chicago. Who'd come up to him after one of his talks. At the U of. All those years ago. Smart kid, articulate young guy, nervously passing his watch from hand to hand as he politely asked a series of questions in the rapidly emptying—

All these years he'd never been able to get this brat out of his head.

And I think you know why, the kid said.

I'm making you with my mind, said my charge.

You're not, the kid said.

You dead? said my charge.

Kid winced.

Sir, is it really the case that the earth is *cooling*? he said, ignoring the question, intent, it seemed, on resuming their previous conversation.

His eyes were, as before, positively piercing.

See, that makes zero sense to me, he said (said again, as he had all those years ago).

Also, he said, hadn't there been *studies*?

Here it came, thought my charge.

Ah, Christ, here it came (again).

Studies your own company did? the kid said. And didn't those studies indicate that the earth was, in fact, heating up, due to human activity? And didn't you come to know about those studies? And didn't your company, on the basis of those studies, redesign your offshore drilling rigs to accommodate the seas that you, from those studies, knew would be rising?

I don't know of any studies of the type you're mentioning, my charge said stiffly.

A murmur of discontent ran through the crowd.

There was also a memo, the kid said. You oil pigs got together and planned the whole thing out, didn't you? Deny, delay, obfuscate. You were all in on it. But you—you led it. You were the leader of the liars.

Well, the kid hadn't said *that* in Chicago.

I'm saying it *now*, the kid said. I know about it *now*. In my current state, I know a *lot*. I know *exactly* who you are, and *everything* you did.

My charge felt the urge to shut it down. By walking off in the abrupt, purposely dismissive way he'd developed over many years of telegraphing displeasure to absolute nobodies.

But couldn't move. The kid just stood there, glaring.

He had to fight.

Fight this crap.

Look, first off, he said. Nobody'd told him a thing about any studies.

The crowd erupted in laughter.

No, come on, think about it: Was he, as CEO, supposed to know every single detail about every minor bit of research ever done, at even the lowest levels of the company, one of the largest companies in the world, by the way, if not *the* largest, as well as (thank you very much) consistently the most profitable? Or did he, perhaps, have a good number of other, more important things to worry about?

Therefore, he'd had no idea—zero—about those studies. Zilch. About which so many were now blabbing such absolute crap.

The silence of the kid and the hundreds of thousands of gathered dead made the falseness of this statement uncomfortable even to him.

Well, okay, yes, fine. What did they think he was, an idiot? The kind of dillweed whose underlings would dare fail to brief him on studies that had a direct bearing on his business? The kind of manager who'd tolerate being left in the dark? Jesus, yes, of course he'd known about those studies, he'd read them cover to cover, as was his responsibility, but he'd been under no fiduciary obligation whatsoever to disclose/publicize such studies, if, in fact, such studies even—

Oh, he knew how it looked.

It looked like he'd known.

Known all along.

Lied about it publicly while privately taking such actions as necessary to protect the firm's—

Well, Jesus Christ, it hadn't been just him. Had it? Hell, no. What about Sawyer, what about Edwards and Chen and Archbold and Keaton? What about R. D. Smitts, Velasco, Purdy, Diamond, Trencher, Filipi? What about Wendell Boot, Tammy Whitman? What about that crowd? What about the guys/gals from the other big operations? Malcolm Handy at Centoil, Brian Haster at Globaco/Bexi? They knew, they all knew, they had research departments of their own, their names were all on that goddamn API memo.

A gust of something like panic swept over my charge.

Had he?

"Lied"?

Lied, then?

In a sense?

If viewed from a certain—

Ah, fuck it, what did it matter now, what a former waitress and a punk with a bad suit and a bunch of sprites or ghosts or whatnot thought of him? He'd be dead soon. And free. Free of this body. As he'd been when young. When young you were free of your body because it only brought you pleasure. He remembered clearing a chain-link fence in one go; swimming from dusk to dawn, breaking only for lunch; racing up a flight of stairs at Yost Field House, back down, up again, just because he could; diving into Crow Creek, zero fear; helping Denise and Rick Whoever move into their place on Wanamaker: crossing the lawn singing "Que Sera, Sera" at the top of his lungs, a box of records on his head, bottle of beer in one hand, window shade in the other.

Soon he'd be powerful like that again.

He just had to get out of this body.

And with this he began seeking death, opening himself eagerly up to it, seeing it as the end of something difficult: not his whole life (which had been wonderful) but just this last phase of it, and not even this whole last day, no, just this evening, and not even the whole evening, just the part of it that began when I came here and started filling his mind with doubts about who he was and what he'd done.

But that was finished now and the next phase was about to begin.

This fellow here—who once, though small, had been kind of wonderful-looking, with thick blond hair that went nearly white in summer and snappy little muscles—this fellow here (with a hump on his back now, and patches of terrible-looking eczema all over, and chest muscles that swung like sausages as he dried his feet with a towel)—this fellow here (with a tumor the size of a grape right here behind this eye, a tumor still growing, even now)—this ugly old conglomeration of flesh was going away (like the planks in the floor of his childhood home, like the glass in the windows and the shingles on the roof), and also going away was the flesh-wad in his noggin that had, all these years, been making the thoughts, feelings, and beliefs that had made *him*, and soon there'd be nothing but a big empty field where his beloved childhood home had been and nothing but a stiff moldering hunk of irrelevant meat left of what had once been the great K.J.—

As for anything he might've done "wrong"—

Yes? I said.

I got swept up, he said.

In? I said.

Me, he said. Myself.

Goodness.

But what else could I have done, he said.

He was speaking, in his crude way, of *elevation* itself.

True, it was only in his head (a mere idea, not yet visceral or urgent).

But his was a formidable intelligence and could cover vast amounts of ground quickly.

Don't give up, I said. You're on to something.

Am I, he said.

Say goodbye to it, I said. Goodbye to the self. That's all you need to—

Not so fast, ladybug, he said.

There was something he needed me to know.

First off:

Nobody could know what it was like, being him.

Nobody.

How delicious, how perfect.

Nobody.

Though physically he might have been in Texas, he'd actually been everywhere. People in Paris knew of him, and Dubai and Berlin and Cape Town, and would refer to him by his whole name: K. J. Boone.

What's K. J. Boone going to think of that?

We have to consider the whole K. J. Boone of it all. Don't we?

They did.

They surely did.

To be him was to be always the biggest fish in a sea of substantial fish. At a shareholders' meeting, or up at the Capitol, or out on a swanky veranda at some conference center in the Alps. All that power, all that money, all those massed experiences gazing up at him, awaiting his words. He had something to offer; they needed him. He spoke easily, with authority, was charming, in his way; he persuaded, left people feeling his way was the best way. He presented powerfully (if humbly), but it was more than that. What he was, they were not, and would never be; where he'd been, they hadn't been (and couldn't go); what he knew, they'd never know.

So they turned to him, trusted him, feared him, even.

Only a handful of people in all of history had ever known that kind of power. Presidents, maybe, depending on the era; kings, sure, but their kingdoms were not worldwide; movie stars and such, but that was all superficial crap. He spoke and markets moved; called a king and the king picked up. He'd decided we were sticking with oil and, goddamn it, we'd stuck with oil and the world got twenty, thirty good years in exchange.

You're welcome.

You're welcome, world.

Goodbye, beloved hunk of rock, overrun of late with jabbering moronic ingrates.

His enemies could have it, the whole damn thing.

Every last one of them could freeze to death while starving in the dark.

He was going home now, to God, his dear God, who'd always loved and protected him and made good things, all the best things, happen for him. Thank you, Lord, thank you for making me who I was and not some little squirming powerless nincompoop.

Thank you for making me unique, one of a kind, incomparable, victorious.

For making me *me*.

This guy.

This guy right here.

Over and out.

Uh-oh, I thought.

It's hooey, pure hooey, he said, turning on me with surprising force, given the negligible trace of life left in him. You're a hooey-pusher. A false prophet. Anybody *ever* buy that *elevation* crap? You ever actually sold anybody on that line of bull? What a snore. Not for me, thanks. When I win, I dance. When I lose? Also dance. I dance the dance called: next time, fuckers. Goodbye forever, lady. You lost. You blew it. You comforted me not one iota. And I want you to know that.

He was like a deflated balloon in which, despite all external appearances, there remained one last bit of air.

Or vitriol.

Or spite.

With which someone could yet be hurt.

If he just put his mind to it.

But then a sudden look of warmth passed over his face.

Do you remember, he said.

Remember what? I said gently.

(Perhaps a change of heart? We had, after all, been through so much together.)

That salamander, he said.

Sorry? I said.

That angel food cake, he said.

I'm not your mother, I said.

I felt a presence behind me, and turned, and there she was:

A country woman, of our ilk, taken aback to find herself in such a grand house, surprisingly tall, taller than he'd dreamed her up earlier.

She approached timidly, head down, as if afraid she might say something that would, at this fraught moment, harm or confuse him.

Will you excuse us? she said.

I withdrew.

Withdrew from the orb of his thoughts.

She knelt beside the bed with some difficulty, arthritic from all those years of farm- and housework.

What song is this? she said and hummed a little tune.

"Bluebird Lane," said my charge.

Remember that table in your room? she said.

You painted it red, he said.

With gold trim, she said.

I'm dying, he said.

Oh, my boy, she said.

Then she spoke to him so softly I couldn't hear.

But he was, it seemed, comforted.

I edged back into the orb of his thoughts and confirmed it.

Yes.

All was well, he felt. He was off the hook. His mother'd just said as much.

There'd been some sort of misunderstanding here lately, he felt her to have said. Lots of mean talk and allegations and strange idiots showing up at the last minute. But he'd done nothing wrong. On the contrary, he'd always been a good boy, who'd become a good man, and had gone out and done all sorts of interesting things that she and her people, and his father and his people, being poor folks, had never had a chance to do. That made a mother proud. Yes, it did.

So, no: he'd done nothing wrong.

At all.

On the contrary.

He should go on now, to glory.

Are you in glory? he asked.

She smiled uncertainly, got slowly to her feet.

Someday, she said. Maybe. But one such as you? Should just go right on ahead.

He began truly dying.

His mind was no longer accessible to me; he was no longer thinking, not in the conventional sense, had begun the transition, was merging with all-that-is, leaving the husk of himself behind, becoming something both more and less than he had ever been before.

His wife, sensing what was happening, rose.

Their daughter rose too.

The two of them stepped forward on either side of his mother.

Wife, mother, daughter stood there in a row. Then his father returned. Still raw from their earlier encounter, he lingered in the doorway in the familiar country slouch. My charge's eyes went to him. His father raised a hand in greeting, the hand short a finger. Then he grew timid, brought it down, raised the other, undamaged hand.

My charge understood this gesture to mean: We've had our differences, son, but you did big stuff, and if I, even by way of certain errors I made, contributed to that, well sir, I consider myself lucky to have been a part of that whole deal, truly.

You did us proud, said his mother.

And how, said his father.

Go on to glory, said his mother.

Then his mother went over, hungrily embraced his father, put her mouth greedily on his, and the two became one.

And it was over.

My charge's wife (now widow) stepped up, smoothed his hair, kissed his head, took his two already-stiffening hands into her own and kissed them, left first, then right.

You did good, she said.

So good, the daughter said.

We love you and appreciate you, said his wife, in a voice louder than her usual speaking voice.

Amazing. It was always amazing.

Goodbye, goodbye, I thought, and then: Ah, hello.

Out of my charge's body leaned my charge.

In spirit form now, of our ilk.

He rose from the bed, experiencing, as we all did at first, the suddenly less onerous influence of gravity, glanced at his wife and daughter, then looked over at me, puzzled.

And the Mels burst in.

At last, said G.

Long damn wait, said R.

They had with them a thick, coarse rope, which they wove between his legs, up over one shoulder, then around his waist. They cinched it tight and secured the arrangement with a tremendous rusty lock for which, I somehow knew, no key existed.

He'll fight it at first, said G.

But in time, said R.

He'll settle, said G.

Be broken, said R.

And together, we'll roam the earth, encouraging former compatriots in their final moments, said G.

As we have encouraged him, said R.

Tonight, said G.

Only one side's right, said R.

Our side, said G.

Otherwise, what? said R.

We were wrong? said G.

All along? said R. The totality of our life's work a big bleck?

Every one of our life-moments spent in the service of utter doo-doo? said G.

Can't have that, said R.

Won't, said G.

Must remain entirely certain, said R.

At the risk of, said G.

We won't say at the risk of *what*, said R.

The more we work to convince ourselves, the more convinced we'll stay, said G.

And the more convinced we stay, the less likely we are to consider, said R.

What might await us, said G.

Were we to even briefly become less convinced, said R.

Of the rightness of our cause, said G.

And by that, we win, said R.

We win, we win, said G.

Come along, said R.

Come along, little dog, said G. Who formerly commanded us.

My charge looked at me imploringly. Having by now intuited the way things worked in this realm, he (still roped) lunged into me, having, I could tell, something he urgently wished to communicate.

I held steady, heard him out.

Because he was no longer so fixedly himself, his diction was altered, although his voice, there in my mind, by way of his thoughts, sounded much the same as it had when he was alive (same flat Wyoming vowels, same faint, acquired Texas accent).

His exit from his body had lessened his reflexive defensiveness.

The magnitude of his sins was now painfully clear to him.

He had not yet reacquired overt speech.

However:

The thing can yet be fixed (was the gist). It can. And I know just how. Am I not ideally suited? For the mighty effort that must now come? If all is to be put to rights? It will, I assure you, be easily done, if led by me. Clean seas, green grass, white shirts blowing on a line in a pure wind. All of that will be. Again. If only you let me lead the thing. It is easily done. Not *easily* (elbow grease required, sure, a ton of it) but *straightforwardly.* Once the truth gets into a fellow, all becomes easy. After that it's just work, work, work, at which (there can be no doubt on your part, sister, having come, tonight, to know me) I am a master. Who better than me? I broke it, I'll fix it. Easy as pie. It will take some time (not much). For me to acquaint myself. With the methods. That will best suit. Wind, sun, nukes? Some way of reclaiming/purifying? There are so many possibilities once the mind allows them. I shall command the mighty levers. As is natural to me. I did no wrong. Yet wrong was done. By me. And yet: no blame. Blame dissipates the energy of the doing. We must fix, only fix. Fix, fix, fix.

He was still within me, I was still within him; I spoke gently back:

Too late, I said.

Too late? he said.

Afraid so, I said.

The violence with which the Mels dragged him out of the room and propelled him down the stairs (even as he protested that to take him now, when the solution was so clear to him, was insane, was an outrage, was a terrible crime against the world) seemed, to me, excessive.

But there was nothing to be done about it.

I moved away, to the window.

The wedding was winding down. Guests were piling into shuttle buses, which rolled away down the street, headlights coming on, going off, coming back on again. There were shouts, bits of off-pitch singing, promises to meet again. On the front lawn the bride and groom (drunk) were bidding a digressive goodbye to a (sober) group from the mother of the bride's church. A few spare children, exhaustion-delirious, dodged in and out of a hedge, one of them with a tail-resembling napkin tucked into the back of his pants.

Through the crowd, unseen by them, came the Mels, dragging my charge along on his stomach. Though still resisting, he was swiftly being converted by the pain and shock of it to acquiescence. He requested that they stop, please, stop dragging him, he'd walk, he'd willingly walk. They stopped. He got to his feet, and the Mels set off at a rapid pace, him stumbling along behind on the rope, the tenor of his resistance softening into pleading.

Behind him followed his mother and his father, separate beings again, not speaking to each other. Soon, I knew, their paths would diverge and, forgetting about him entirely, they would wander off separately, to seek their respective solutions to whatever kept them bound in this realm.

Up above, the sky was full of those collective regional dead, fleeing the death-room, dispersing back to the fields, yards, offices, and nooks between buildings in which each normally, fitfully and unhappily, resided.

The moon was the highest it had been all night.

A single cloud moved slowly past it.

Two pronghorns of our ilk were tightly, repetitively circling my charge's mailbox, this being the place where, hundreds of years before, they had been killed in successive months by the same mountain lion, who, nearby, staggered around in eternal reenactment of its last moments, having choked to death on the haunch of the second.

It was hard, this life.

Poor regional dead, stuck here, confused and discontent.

Poor pronghorns, who'd died so scared.

Poor mountain lion, ditto.

This life would, for no reason, smash its big fist down into this or that face, no apologies. While the rest of the world watched, then moved happily on.

Including my face.

I'd gotten blown up.

ME.

Lloyd had remarried quick, gone on to have kids, three kids. After his death, he'd fled this realm without so much as a goodbye. My dipshit killer had lived to a ripe old age, having forgiven himself.

A nice girl had been born and lived and loved and all that and then got killed for no reason by some random dumbass and all her plans and dreams were just gone.

And the world completely forgot about her, like she'd never even *been*.

It was sad, so harsh.

Just cruel.

I couldn't stand it.

The Mels, for fun, gave the rope a hard yank. My charge fell with a cry to his knees.

Was there nothing to be done about all this suffering?

Elevation flared within me.

My charge had been born *him*. But had never *chosen* to be born him. That had just *happened* to him. Then life had happened to that *him*, exerting upon it certain deleterious effects, including but not limited to: the powerful nature of his early desires, which had led him to *strive*, which, in turn, led him to *accomplish*, and, in *accomplishing*, he had brought about *harm*, even as the mind he'd been given, from the start, bloomed forth, just as it must, causing him, in the face of that harm (and the accusations made against him due to that harm), to suppress and deny the reality of the harm and become, over time, averse to even acknowledging it.

It had all unscrolled just as it must.

It did not seem strange to me, but *inevitable*.

An *inevitable occurrence* upon which it would be ludicrous to pass judgment.

And yet judgment was being passed.

Most harshly.

I leapt out the window and down I swooped, through one Mel and then the other, thinking, as I did, of *hacking, slicing:* a knife *ripping* through a watermelon, an ax *splitting* a log.

When I came out on the other side, the Mels and my charge had been lacerated into thick sections, which, after a few microseconds of confusion, began reforming into the Mels and my charge.

The rope, because inanimate, remained cut.

My charge stumbled away, putting some prohibitive distance between himself and the Mels.

I *whisked* through one Mel, then the other, imagining, this time, that they were empty vessels, with openings in the tops of their heads, and that two streams of wet concrete were pouring in, one per Mel, instantly hardening.

I came out on the other side, looked back, and there they were: legs splayed, sitting side by side, heavy as could be, like statues, Mel G. leaning slightly off to the right, Mel R. to the left. Because their arms were made of stone, they were unable to catch themselves as they tipped (G. to the right, R. to the left).

Unfair, said G., from there on his side, slightly cracked.

Manifestly unfair, said R.

We waited all night for him, said G.

Twelve years I waited for him, said R.

Nine years I waited, said G.

You can't do that, said R.

You can't just do that, said G.

And yet I did, I said. I just now did it.

Who are you? said R.

What are you? said G.

Who and what are you, anyway? said R.

For me to know and you to find out, I said.

It served those two doofuses right for always being so crappy and mean to everybody.

Suck eggs and die, creepos, I said.

I *whisked* through them once more, imagining the concrete turning to water.

And it did.

Coughing and gagging, they hustled away, cursing me but only under their breaths, so terrified were they of my new capabilities.

Madame! the Frenchman shouted from somewhere.

I looked up.

Here he came, falling fast.

What are you doing? he said. What in the world have you—

He hit the lawn, dropped through, seconds later bobbed back up and was standing next to me, smelling fresh (lilac scent, beeswax pomade, touch of lye soap).

Now what? he said angrily. What is your plan, *madame*? For this fellow you have so recklessly freed? Did he not rightly belong with those two beasts? It is terrible, what you have done. *C'est une erreur tragique.* You and your terrible, facile ideas! According to which, anyone may do anything. Anything at all. All is instantly forgiven, no matter what. Tell me, do you believe it? Really believe it? Bad and good are the same? Damage does no harm? The guilty are innocent, the sinner and the saint shall both sit at the right hand of the Father, enjoying equal portions?

You don't know what you're talking about, I said.

The Frenchman looked at me as if I were a stranger, wholly unknowable to him.

You have freed a monster, he said.

My charge stumbled over, still incapable of speech, and knelt at the Frenchman's feet.

To understand his intentions, I knelt down too, side-scooched in. The Frenchman, for the same purpose, bent at the waist, thrust his head into the headspace of my charge.

Let me go with you (was the gist of my charge's plea). To visit those others like us. Who have sinned against the earth and find themselves at the point of death. And, with you, urge them to repent. As you, honorably, urged me to do.

All of us (charge, Frenchman, Jill, non-Jill) were there messily within one another, our minds abuzz with one another's thoughts.

A change was coming over the Frenchman. He had despised my charge, been frustrated by him, had at times wished him harm, did, indeed, consider him monstrous. But the transformation my charge was undergoing was reminding the Frenchman of the transformation he himself had undergone all those years ago, at his end, or, more precisely, just after it, while lying in his coffin in a stifling Parisian parlor, surrounded by his wife, children, and scientific colleagues, all of whom had loved him dearly and were still trying to grasp that this great man, who, through his genius, had altered the world, removing the necessity for so much dehumanizing toil, was now leaving them forever.

In that moment, amid sounds of praise and weeping, time had stopped and he had been flung forward by some irresistible force through the decades and shown the potential comprehensive effect of that which he had invented.

With that, his peace had ended and his all-consuming quest had begun.

You are wrong to be so hard on yourself, I said. You were, after all, *inevitable*. An *inevitable occurrence*. Who else could you have been but who you—

No, the Frenchman said crisply. No, no, no. That rubbish is not for me.

And turned his attention to my charge.

Do you have any idea of where we might profitably go first? he said, still bent at the waist, head still within the head of my charge. To whom?

My charge cocked his head, as if surveying the entire world. Nodded.

The Frenchman and I instantly knew who he had in mind: a former competitor of his in Santa Barbara, with less than a day to live and many things for which to atone.

So, we go, the Frenchman said. *Allons-y.*

My charge rose from his knees and, dressed as he'd so often dressed for work (black suit, white shirt, green tie), began patting his pockets frantically, as if searching for his wallet. He tightened the knot of his tie, checked the time (but was wearing no watch), all of this communicating an urgent desire to be about his business, then looked down in consternation at his feet (which were bare).

Now, as if trying to divest himself of all memories of this time and place that might inhibit him in the next phase of his activities, he gave his head a brisk shake, as a horse will do, and started off at a fast clip (the way he used to when leaving his office, so as not to be detained or interfered with by mere underlings) along the road before his house, and then began to walk faster, then jog, and by the time he reached the margin of the forest bordering the neighborhood and swerved off into it, he was running at a full sprint, faster, by far, than he had ever run in life, even when young, strong, and at his best, wincing at the pain this extraordinary pace was causing his bare feet (and would continue to cause them into a vast, interminable future, hundreds of years long at least, likely longer, possibly forever).

While the Frenchman flew supportively along above.

Then they were gone.

No matter how many of the dying these two might convert, the effect on the world would be, I knew, negligible, since the dying were *over,* their potential for *doing* anything at all essentially nil.

And yet, what else was there for them to do, but whatever they felt they still might?

With no charge in my care, I began, as usual, to wane.

Gravity became ever less compelling, my clothes began to fade, reappear, fade away again. My hearing grew acute, allowing me to track my charge's progress through the forest by the rustling sounds made by the various animals (a white-tailed deer, two gray foxes, a rafter of wild turkeys) he startled in passing.

Becoming ever less substantial, thereby less bound to any one place, I extended myself outward and saw that, yes, even this, this humble swath of Texas forest, was *less,* less than the forests of my bygone days: dead trees leaned against sick trees popping with fungal blooms, the forest floor repellently thick with mounds of dry pine needles. Underground, the strands of the root system ran black; the canopy above was perilously thin;

the leaves of the ashes and dogwoods seemed brittle, as if they might shatter at the slightest touch.

Oh, it was true, all true, what Mr. Bhuti had said, and discouraging beyond measure:

This lovely old place, ruined forever, maybe.

One last time I shot up, then passed through the second-story wall of the death room (farewell bed, weeping wife, stunned daughter; farewell corpse, hands newly wife-crossed upon the (no-longer-heaving) chest) and blasted up through the ceiling.

Ascending to the tip of the tallest of the five cupola-topping finials, balancing atop it on one foot, I regarded the nearly empty wedding-yard below (wineglass in a flower bed, napkin in the pool, besotted couple slow-dancing to no music at all), the sleepy neighborhood, the flat, flat, light-flecked city of Dallas.

Something was bothering me.

I had perhaps overstepped by my intervention vis-à-vis the Mels.

I'd been, tell the truth, pretty darn rough on them.

And weren't they also *inevitable*? *Inevitable occurrences*? Upon which, therefore, it would be impossible, even ludicrous, to pass judgment? And hadn't I just passed judgment on them? Quite harshly? By lacerating them into sections, hollowing them out, then filling them with concrete, and all of that?

Well, sure.

I mean, I guess I'd kind of dropped the ball on that one.

Therein lay the danger of existing out of *elevation*.

Of retaining even a trace of one's former self:

One's pity became constricted.

One judged, one preferred; one acted and, in acting, erred.

One screwed the pooch, felt crappy about it later.

So:

The time had come for me to be frank with myself, with that dual *we;* to say, to that sweet, treasured-but-harmful Jill-portion that lingered within me still, that *we* were finished, and *I* must go on without her.

Yes, yes, she seemed to say, I get it, I get that. But just don't forget me.

But forgetting her was exactly what I meant to do.

Centralizing my considerable strength, I exploded upward, holding in my heart the intention of returning to that distant place to which those of our ilk must return when in need of a fresh beginning.

And soon enough was there:

Hurtling toward "Paul Bowman," who was, as always when I sought a fresh beginning, luminous, spectral, celestial, the size of a mountain, seated at that same (football field–sized) metal table, nervously smoking.

It was, each time, a fresh gamble.

One ran the risk of being rebuffed, and finding oneself consigned to that realm from which no further positive action would ever be possible.

(It had never happened to me yet.

But one never knew.)

Passing directly into this mountainous spectral Bowman, I came, again, to know rather too much about him:

Over me washed a feeling that no one *got* me, no one *liked* me, I could always tell from the first minute I met someone, by that snot-assed look on his or her face, like, Ugh, no no no, get away from me, dirtbag, pronto.

And so on.

And then:

Gradually he came to seem, if I may say it this way, *inevitable*.

An *inevitable occurrence*, upon which, therefore, it would be impossible, even ludicrous, to pass judgment.

Who else could he have been but who he was?

At what moment could he have become other than he became?

I felt a familiar, powerful truth being beamed into me by a vast, beneficent God, in the form of this unyielding directive:

Comfort.

Comfort, for all else is futility.

Blessed by this, I fell.

Willed myself to fall.

Fell farther.

Acquiring, as I did, arms, hands, legs, feet, all of which, as usual, became more substantial with each passing second.

Below, it was winter.

Yes: dark night, dead of winter, a silent valley, and, on a small rise, a neat little cabin, orange-lit from within.

I observed all this as I plummeted past and then my feet pierced a snowbank and I continued down through the ice-crust of a frozen pond and found myself upright and vertical, ten feet or so below the surface.

There were fish in this pond, even now, in winter, swimming, but slowly.

Interesting.

I found myself both fully and consistently clothed:

Beige skirt, pale pink blouse, black pumps.

Not unthawed in the least.

Well, that would come. I need only wait.

I waited.

A woman was dying in that cabin. Somehow I knew it was a woman.

I felt again the old, familiar, generalized fondness:

She had not willed herself into this world and was now being taken out of it by force, the many subsystems within her that had always given her so much satisfaction shutting down agonizingly.

Soon *it* would come, accompanied by disbelief and panic, and she would find herself on the wrong side of a rapidly closing door, everything she had ever known and loved out of reach, over *there*, beyond it.

At such moments, I especially cherished my task.

I could comfort.

I could.

Thank you, thank you, I whispered.

And vowed to seek *elevation* forevermore.

About the Author

George Saunders is the author of thirteen books, including the novel *Lincoln in the Bardo,* which won the Man Booker Prize, and five collections of stories, including *Tenth of December,* which was a finalist for the National Book Award, and the recent collection *Liberation Day* (selected by former President Obama as one of his ten favorite books of 2022). Three of Saunders's books—*Pastoralia, Tenth of December,* and *Lincoln in the Bardo*—were chosen for *The New York Times*'s list of the 100 Best Books of the 21st Century. Saunders hosts the popular Story Club on Substack, which grew out of his book on the Russian short story, *A Swim in a Pond in the Rain.* In 2013, he was named one of the world's 100 Most Influential People by *Time* magazine. He teaches in the creative writing program at Syracuse University.

About the Type

This book was set in Fournier, a typeface named for Pierre-Simon Fournier (1712–68), the youngest son of a French printing family. He started out engraving woodblocks and large capitals, then moved on to fonts of type. In 1736 he began his own foundry and made several important contributions in the field of type design; he is said to have cut 147 alphabets of his own creation. Fournier is probably best remembered as the designer of St. Augustine Ordinaire, a face that served as the model for the Monotype Corporation's Fournier, which was released in 1925.